About the Author

Helen C Burke was born in Drogheda, County Louth in Ireland, and now lives in Kent with her husband. Passionate about writing, *Billy's Search for the Unspell Spell* is the sequel, to her debut book *Billy's Search for the Healing Well*. A mother of three adult children and a grandmother of four, Helen worked for her local Adult Education Authority before retiring to travel and improve her writing skills.

Billy's Search for the Unspell Spell

Helen C. Burke

Billy's Search for the Unspell Spell

Olympia Publishers

London

www.olympiapublishers.com
OLYMPIA PAPERBACK EDITION

Copyright © Helen C. Burke 2020

The right of Helen C. Burke to be identified as author of
this work has been asserted in accordance with sections 77 and 78 of the
Copyright, Designs and Patents Act 1988.

All Rights Reserved

No reproduction, copy or transmission of this publication
may be made without written permission.
No paragraph of this publication may be reproduced,
copied or transmitted save with the written permission of the publisher,
or in accordance with the provisions
of the Copyright Act 1956 (as amended).

Any person who commits any unauthorised act in relation to
this publication may be liable to criminal
prosecution and civil claims for damage.

A CIP catalogue record for this title is
available from the British Library.

ISBN: 978-1-78830-377-4

This is a work of fiction.
Names, characters, places and incidents originate from the writer's
imagination. Any resemblance to actual persons, living or dead, is purely
coincidental.

First Published in 2020

Olympia Publishers
Tallis House
2 Tallis Street
London
EC4Y 0AB

Printed in Great Britain

Dedication

To my beautiful grandchildren,
George, Elliott, Bridie and Ryan.
With much love always
Your Nana x

Introduction

Billy tittered at Ginger Nick who was tearing down the street dodging the sharp needles of rain. Turning from the wet, grey day outside he sat on the new James Bond rug, and pulled a wooden box from under his bed. Slowly, he opened the lid, and touched the crystal bottle inside. He still had terrible nightmares about Finbar, the fearsome Rat Boy. He'd see his sharp teeth, his beady eyes, and his wiry whiskers. Sometimes, he'd even wake up at night, sure he was scuttling across the bedroom floor.

He was lucky to have his mum home though. She was the reason he'd run away to Ireland in the first place. Within a week of drinking the water from the Healing Well, she was unhooked from the bleeping, hospital machinery and sent home.

'It's like a miracle,' the consultant had said, and to Billy's delight, they hadn't gone home but had stayed in his gran's cosy little house.

At first his mum was upset that his gran was so ill, she'd stayed behind in Ireland. Now, though, she was furious because instead of coming home when she was well, his gran had swanned off to Peru, somewhere in South

America. 'She obviously doesn't give a fig about us,' Mum had fumed when the first bright postcard had dropped through the letter box nine months ago. Postcards arrived every month after that, all with a hastily scribbled *'love, Gran'*, but never with any news of when she was coming home.

'I don't understand why she's stayed away for so long,' Mum said sadly, after the sixth postcard arrived. 'Maybe she has a boyfriend,' said Billy, making her laugh.

Billy knew his gran wasn't in Peru! If only she'd shared her secret with his mum, his life would be so much easier. Before his mum was born, his gran was a flower fairy. Which, even though it sounded ridiculous was true. After the evil Rat Boys chased the fairies from the Magical Meadow, in Glendalough, Erin, (his gran) had begged the Merrow to turn her into a human so she could marry his grandpops (Shane). The Merrow had agreed, but had warned her that the spell would be broken if she ever returned to Ireland. Erin and Shane were married in England, and a year later Billy's mum, Caitlin, was born.

Last year, when Billy's mum was very sick, he'd run away to Ireland, to find the Healing Well that Gran had mentioned in her stories. The story was, that all who drank or bathed in the well's magical water would be cured. Unfortunately, when his gran had followed him, she'd broken the Merrow's spell. It was all his fault that she was now fluttering around Glendalough with little silvery wings.

'Come in, come in, you're soaking wet,' Billy heard his mum open the front door. Feet thundered up the stairs, and a pair of blue eyes peeped around the corner. 'What ya doing?' asked Jimmy, his friend, from next door.

'Might play on the PlayStation,' said Billy, unenthusiastically. Today, he was missing Gran more than ever.

'Oh no, not again. That's so boring,' whined Emma, Jimmy's twin sister, who stood, dripping wet beside him.

'Got any better ideas?' asked Billy, nodding to the rain beating against the bedroom window.

'Yeah, tell us a scary story about the Rat Boys, Finbar, and Erin, the Fairy Queen.' Emma's blonde pigtails pinged up and down, as she flopped on to the bed.

'Yeah, that's a good idea' said Jimmy, flopping down beside her. 'How'd ya find the Healing Well again?'

Billy sighed, knowing that once the twins started asking questions they never stopped.

'With Captain Nealy's map,' he told them, for the hundredth time.

'Did the water from the Healing Well really make your mum better?' they asked together, as they often did.

'Might've, I dunno,' shrugged Billy, knowing they didn't believe a word he said.

'Is that the crystal bottle you filled with healing water?' Emma gazed at the sparkling bottle in the box.
'I'm hungry,' said Billy rudely, and snapping the lid shut, he headed for the door

Chapter 1
The Meadowers

The rain had stopped lashing down at last, and crossing the road the children stood gawping at the shabby house opposite.

'What's happened to Ratty?' Jimmy wondered out loud. They'd called their neighbour 'Ratty,' because of his wiry whiskers, and beady eyes, and because of the way he'd scuttled like a rat. They were sure he must have a tail too, because weirdly, his surname, *Nimrev,* spelled *'vermin',* backwards.

'He disappeared about the same time as your gran. Maybe he's her secret boyfriend,' Emma giggled.

'No way!' snapped Billy knowing Nimrev was a Rat Boy who'd spied on his gran.

Captured by Finbar, when he'd run away to Ireland, Billy had watched a Rat Boy shedding his fur. Clump, by clump it had fallen to the ground, and suddenly, there was his neighbour Ratty Nimrev, wearing nothing but a smirk. Then sprouting wiry whiskers, sticky out teeth, and a long, black tail, he'd pulled his fur up, like a onesie, and scuttled away with the other rats.

'She's only joking,' said Jimmy, annoyed with Billy for snapping at Emma.

'Well, Ratty's not my gran's boyfriend,' Billy insisted.

'Sssshh! Looks like he's back,' the twins were distracted by a steaming mug on the table, through the window.

'Come on Billy, you're not scared are ya?' Jimmy, was surprised to see him backing away. After all, Billy had given Ratty more cheek than anyone. Billy shook his head and putting on a brave face he crept up the mossy pathway.

A round, unshaven man yanked open the front door as they pressed their noses to the window.

'Clear off, you nosy kids make my life a misery,' he barked.

'You're a chicken,' Jimmy called, as Billy scooted across the road. 'Emma didn't run away, and she's a girl.'

'He looked like Ratty,' puffed Billy, his face bright red.

'What?! No, he didn't. What's wrong with you. You weren't scared of Ratty before.' Jimmy was confused.

Embarrassed to have run away, Billy stormed off in a huff.

'Please, can we go to Ireland?' he asked his mum who was peeling vegetables over the kitchen sink.

'What's brought this on?' she put down the peeler.

'Perlease'—it's just not the same here without Gran.'

'I miss her too, you know. We'd go to Peru, if only I knew where to find her.' She smiled.

'She might come to Ireland for a holiday too.' Billy's fingers were crossed behind his back.

'I'll give her a piece of my mind, if she does,' said mum, sweeping her light brown hair from her face.

'So, we can go then?' Billy's face lit up.

'Well, a holiday might take your mind off things,' she gave him a hug.

Wearing a big cheesy grin Billy stepped into the garden. He couldn't believe his mum was taking him to Ireland, for a holiday. Following the winding path that Gran called 'the curly road,' he wandered around the wide cherry tree, waded through the tall daisies, and hopped on to the patio.

'Anyone in there?' he whispered, tapping on the smallest flower pot.

'Billy, why are you talking to a flower pot?'

'Er, er, I wasn't. I was just looking for my ball' he stammered, surprised to see his mum right behind him.

'Hmmm,' your gran always acted shifty too, whenever she was out here in her Magical Meadow.' Putting down the washing basket, she almost crushed a tiny fairy, who was thirstily, lapping rain drops from a flower petal. Alarmed, the fairy fluttered over Billy's head.

'You don't believe the garden is magical, do you?' Billy was watching the fairy fluttering around in the daisy patch, while his mum was pegging out the washing.

'Of course I believe it's a magical garden. Why else would the flowers bloom here all year round' his mum winked.

A tiny orange haired man suddenly sprang from the flower pot, and kicking Billy hard in the shin, he sprang inside again.

'What's wrong?' his mum's blue eyes widened, as he winced in pain.

'Er, I must've stung myself,' he said, glaring at the flower pot.

'Let me see' she rolled down his sock to check the imaginary sting.

'Looks fine to me, I can't see any redness,' she said, puzzled.

Billy pulled up his sock. 'That hurt, Cornelius,' he said, watching his mum go back inside the house.

'Sorry, I didn't mean to kick you so hard.' The chubby, freckle-faced little fellow with bright red hair hopped-up on to the rim. 'Gran sends her love' he added cheerily, staring into Billy's stony face.

'When's Gran coming home? She can't pretend to be in Peru forever.' He was fed up waiting for some good news.

'Have you ever heard of the Unspell spell?' Cornelius, tumbled on to the grass.

'The what spell?' asked Billy.

'The Unspell spell! It's a spell to undo other spells,' he brushed the leaves from his natty, blue tunic.

'You mean it might undo the Merrow's spell, and Gran can come home? That's wicked!' cried Billy, dancing up and down.

'There's just a little catch,' Cornelius warned him.

'Well, what is it?' Billy waited for the little man to check out his reflection in a puddle.

'Clodagh the Merrow, the keeper of the Unspell spell, has vanished,' he mumbled. Using his finger to brush his teeth, he was looking into the puddle.

'That doesn't make any sense. Why does the Merrow need a spell to undo her own spell?' Billy was disappointed.

'The Merrow's spells last a lifetime. However, the Unspell spell was a gift from a Merman, to use for her own protection,' Cornelius explained.

'Well, it's no good if the Merrow's missing. Why can't Beltenor help?' Billy was losing hope of ever seeing his gran again.

Cornelius put up his hands. 'Hey, I'm just the messenger. Besides, Beltenor blames you lot for taking Ronan away in the first place. She still hasn't found another guardian.'

'You mean, she hasn't found a new slave,' scoffed Billy, who remembered the pampered Water Witch very well.

'Who are you talking to now?' Mum was alarmed to see him muttering into thin air.

'Just thinking out loud,' he said, startled by her habit of appearing from nowhere. 'My teacher says it helps to make sense of things.'

'What kind of things?' she frowned.

'Go on, I dare you to tell her about us,' sniggered Cornelius. Then slicking back his orange hair with a golden comb, he vanished into the pot.

'No way, she'll think I'm nuts,' blurted Billy.

'Who'll think you're nuts?' Mum looked around the garden.

'What? Oh, I was just day-dreaming again.'

Cornelius's deep, violet eyes peeped over the pot, and Billy laughed nervously.

Later that afternoon, Ginger Nick and the twins joined Billy to rummage around his gran's shed.

The shelves groaned, under reams of paper, paint palettes, bundles of pencils, and assorted cards, glitters and glues. There were cupboards full of paint pots, brushes, and paints of every colour. Rolls of luxurious fabrics lay beside his gran's clunky, old, sewing machine, and numerous paintings of peculiar fairies, and woodland creatures covered the shed walls.

'Once, I saw the Rainbow Bird wink her turquoise eye,' Emma admired a spectacular painting of a beautiful bird, in the centre of the wall.

'What, I thought she winked at me too,' admitted Jimmy.

'What about you, Billy?' asked Ginger Nick.

'The Rainbow Bird winks at everyone, all the time. You just have to keep watching. Do you want to hear a story about her?' Billy was dying to share his secrets.

'Nah, we've heard it before. The water from the Healing Well cured her wing.' Ginger Nick was studying the bird's patchwork rainbow feathers, and her deep, turquoise eyes.

'No, not that story. The story of how she rescued me, and Patsy, the leprechaun, from the Rat Boys' cave,' said Billy.

The twins giggled; Billy was always exaggerating.

'The Rat Boys captured us and locked us away in a pitch-black cave. Then, the Rainbow Bird swooped into the cave and dropped a flint through the bars. We cut through the rope on the door and hopped on her back. Then with us clinging on to her rainbow feathers, she escaped through the roof, flew over the mountains, and landed on the oak tree in Magical Meadow, where the Tree Spirits live. It was so scary,' said Billy quite seriously.

'Your gran told us lots of stories about the Rat Boys, the Rainbow Bird, and the Tree Spirits. You're making that up,' Emma laughed.

'No, I'm not. They're real, I saw them in Ireland. The Rat Boys can run on two legs, and bash you with a shillelagh. They can talk too, just like me and you. The Tree Spirits are cool though. Especially Tia, she's my friend,' gabbled Billy, sounding quite mad.

Jimmy and Ginger Nick stopped what they were doing.

'Are you nuts?' spluttered Jimmy.

'No, it's true! The Rainbow Bird saved us from the Rat Boys.' Billy wished he'd kept the story to himself.

'It's a fairy story,' said Emma, sure he was joking.

'No, it's the truth. The Rainbow Bird comes from the Magical Meadow in Glendalough. Just like the Meadowers that live in Gran's garden,' Billy insisted without so much as a titter.

'The Meadowers!' repeated the children.

'Are you feeling okay?' Emma felt his forehead.

'Yeah, I'm fine,' he snapped, swiping her hand away.

Suddenly, several little fairies in ballerina tutus came wafting into the shed. Then holding hands, they fluttered around, tickling Billy's face with their silvery wings.

'Stop being weird,' Emma shrieked at Billy, who was giggling and wriggling and slapping his face.

'Please Cornelius! Make them stop it. I know it was you who put them up to this.'

The fairies fluttered their wings faster, and as Billy wriggled like a worm the children stared, wondering if he'd gone mad. Then unable to stand the terrible tickling any longer he shot into the garden.

'Cornelius, who's Cornelius?' cried Jimmy, chasing after him.

'What's all the noise?' Surprised to see the children running wild around the garden, Billy's mum opened the kitchen window.

'Mum, the garden's called the Magical Meadow because leprechauns, pixies and gnomes live in the flower pots, the trees and the hedges,' blurted Billy, pointing out the different places around the garden. 'They're called the Meadowers,' he added, angrily swiping at the invisible fairies. The giggling fairies fluttered away, and unsure what to do, his mum stared at him, speechless.

'Leprechauns, pixies and gnomes?' the children spluttered into their hands. Suddenly, letting out a terrific yell, Billy ran at the flower pot, and booted it from under a shocked Cornelius. 'Ah ha, that'll wipe the grin off your face,' he laughed, as the little trickster landed on his backside with a bump.

'It's not my fault that I see fairies. I was born with the gift of sight,' he explained, realising he must look ridiculous. Unaware of Cornelius pulling funny faces, his mum stared at the perfectly ordinary flower pot.

'That's it, we're off to Ireland, as soon as possible,' she said, closing the window. 'Who's Patsy, the Leprechaun anyway?' asked Ginger Nick, and tittering, Cornelius ducked into the pot.

Chapter 2
The Missing Merrow

The Meadowers hadn't seen a Rat Boy's whisker since the battle in the cave. Free from Finbar and his army at last, they'd cleared the meadow of the grubby half-gnawed bones, and stacks of decaying food. They'd cleared the choking vines from the Palace's jagged turrets and lop-sided balconies, and swept the rubbish from the brook. They'd rid the silver leaved trees of the rat's nests, both inside and out, and then collecting feathers, twigs, pine cones, leaves, and foxes' fur, they'd made furniture, cushions and curtains for their brand-new homes.

Once again, the wildlife surrounded them including the butterflies, the birds and the bees, and for the first time in a year, music, and laughter, rang throughout the Magical Meadow.

Happy to see the Meadowers settled at last, Erin set off on a water chariot, in search of the Merrow. Sailing close to the Merrow's rock, she spotted a little water nymph splashing about in the water.

'Can you tell me where to find the Merrow today?' she asked, politely.

'We haven't seen her for almost a week,' the Nymph shook her head. Erin was disappointed.

'But someone must know where she is.'

'Maybe a fisherman's taken her away,' said a second water Nymph, who was perched on the rock, drying her golden hair.

'Aye, 'twas a fisherman who took the Merrow, before,' agreed the first Nymph, the icy water from her wings showering Erin, as she fluttered away.

Erin sailed around searching high and low, but it was as if the Merrow had disappeared into thin air.

Patsy, the Leprechaun was feeling quite sea sick, as his leaky, old rowing boat was tossed around on the waves. 'There she is,' he whispered, spying the Ghost ship, bobbing on the horizon in the lashing rain. He was hopeful Captain Nealy might know what had happened to the Merrow.

The last time he'd seen the Ghost ship, it had appeared on the upper lake, as if drawn by an invisible hand. The details had filled in slowly, like a developing photograph, until it was complete, and rocking on the water with its sails billowing in the breeze. Patsy grinned, remembering how Billy's hair had stood on end with every ghostly creak, when they'd climbed on board. Now, in broad daylight, reunited with the Captain and its crew, the ship didn't look half as scary.

Shivering uncontrollably, Patsy sailed closer, and leaning over, he grabbed the rope ladder.

'Do ya wanna die? What ya doing drifting about in that leaky old yoke?' Shocked, the Captain grabbed his hand and hauled him on board.

'The Merrow's m m m missing,' Patsy couldn't stop his teeth from chattering. 'W, we, we wondered if ye'd seen her on ye're travels.' The Captain, dressed flamboyantly in a tri-cornered hat, trimmed with red feathers, a white ruffled shirt, black breeches, and a pair of shiny black boots, eyed him up and down. 'Must be important to bring you out in this weather. What do you want with her?' he asked, pinging his diamond-studded eye patch.

'The M, M, Merrow's Unspell spell c,c, could set Erin free,' said Patsy, his teeth still chattering.

The scraggy bearded crew, each wearing a different coloured bandana, moved closer to hear him over the howling wind.

'The munchkin's looking for the Merrow. Well, any of you lot seen her?' the Captain, bellowed as if they were miles away. The pirates grunted among themselves, and then shook their heads.

'Hmmmm, come to think of it, I ain't heard her terrible screeching for a long while. What do ya think's happened to her then?' the Captain stroked his long, black beard.

'Dunno, no one's seen or heard from her in over a week. She usually sits over there.' Patsy pointed out the Merrow's rock, jutting from the sea, as if the Captain didn't know.

'Who'll protect us from the bandits on the Irish Sea now? There aren't many kind-hearted pirates around,' he added quickly, seeing a frown creeping over the Captain's face.

'Don't worry we'll keep a look out for the Merrow,' the Captain called, as Patsy wobbled down the ladder in the howling gale. So much for his concern, he could've offered him a leak free boat for the journey home, thought Patsy.

'Mind how you go munchkin. Now, jump to it, you rabble,' he heard the Captain holler as the crew hauled in the ship's heavy anchor.

'It's useless.' Erin was upset that after searching everywhere, and asking everyone, they still hadn't found out what had happened to the Merrow.

Tia pushed a little Elf forward, who'd been hiding shyly behind the tree.

'My friend Eamon suggests we speak to Witch Whitely,' she said.

'Will she know where to find the Merrow?' Erin smiled at him.

'Witch Whitely has powerful lotions and potions, but she often finds the answers in the flames.' The Elf's ears turned bright pink.

'Where can we find her today.' Ronan was lounging around on a squashy toadstool, eager for something to do.

'You won't find her today, she goes away on holiday every August,' said Eamon.

'On holiday! Where?' Ronan was puzzled, he'd never heard of a witch going on a holiday before.

'Every year, Witch Whitely enjoys a flutter on the Dingle races' said Eamon.

'Just our luck! A gambling witch who likes to holiday in Kerry! When's she back?' Ronan was disappointed.

'Woah, hold your horses,' Eamonn, sniggered at his own joke. Groaning, Ronan, rolled his eyes.

'It's not his fault if the witch is on holiday,' said Tia, fading from sight. Eamon looked at the curled-up toes of his yellow shoes.

'The Brownies of the Boyne might know where to find her,' he mumbled to the blank space where Tia had hovered moments before.

'Are you sure the Brownies aren't on holiday too?' Ronan asked, sarcastically.

'They'll be on the hill of Tara, by the river Boyne,' said Eamon snootily.

'We could fly there on the Rainbow Bird.' Erin's silvery wings were fluttering with excitement.

'A trip! How exciting,' Tia reappeared, making Eamon jump.

'I'm not flying anywhere on that bird, ever again. I'll meet ye at the races,' said Patsy, who was terrified of heights.

'Oh, come on, Patsy. You'll be as safe as houses if you sit between us.' Erin put an arm around his shoulder.

'I'd have gorgeous, shimmery wings like ye, if I was meant to fly. Besides, I'm going somewhere else tomorrow.'

'Why not go afterwards?' asked Erin. Patsy shook his head stubbornly.

'Don't be such a baby,' she teased.

'Okay, okay, anything for a quiet life,' he shrugged.

'Good, now remember to bring plenty of gold. The flutter-huts are open from dawn to dusk.' Erin was very excited about the races.

The next day, with them clinging to her feathers, the Rainbow Bird fluttered into the sky.

'Are you okay?' Ronan asked after a while, noticing how Tia's knuckles had turned white with fear. Tia looked down, her hazel eyes following the river Boyne. Erin wondered again, why Tia hardly spoke to Ronan anymore. It just didn't make sense; she'd adored him since the day he'd jangled on to Brittas Bay beach, in his rusty, old armour. Now, she barely looked at him.

They gasped at the vast, green patchwork below. The rush of the wind took their breath away as the Rainbow Bird sailed over tree tops, mountains and lakes. Finally, descending at an alarming speed, she perched on a stone monument at the top of a hill. Relieved the roller-coaster journey was over, Erin and Tia floated eagerly to the ground.

'Where are we?' Erin's wings sparkled with the early morning dew.

'The Hill of Tara,' said Tia.

Ronan somersaulted to the ground, and turning over and over, he landed on his feet. 'Show off,' muttered Patsy, crashing on his backside.

'There's not a single Brownie in sight,' said Tia, her haunted eyes searching the green fields.

'Who are you looking for?' asked one of six Bownies, standing right behind them. They turned and stared at the Brownies, who were dressed from head to toe in brown.

'Well, has the cat got your tongues? Who are you, and what do you want? The rude Brownie at the front demanded, before they could answer.

Erin began to introduce everyone, but the Brownies were distracted by Tia, who'd disappeared from sight.

'Oh, I'm so sorry, must be the excitement,' she giggled, reappearing like a ghost.

'How annoying,' scoffed the glum-faced Brownie.

'No, not at all, it's sometimes very useful.' Her giggle seemed to annoy him even more.

'Bridie, Breeda, Brian, Bryony, Brendan, and Brucie,' announced the rude Brownie, pointing to himself last.

Amused, Patsy slapped his knee, and giving him a nudge, Ronan quickly explained about the missing Merrow.

'This is disastrous news. The Merrow protects us from the rabble on the sea,' they gabbled at once.

'Don't mention Captain Nealy, whatever you do,' Patsy whispered to Tia.

'I'm sorry it's such upsetting news,' Ronan apologised.

'How long have you known about this?' Brucie was visibly shaken.

'Long enough to have searched all over,' said Ronan.

'You should've come sooner. She must be in some kind of trouble.'

'Ten brownie points Brucie,' scoffed Patsy, fed up of his rudeness. 'Are you making fun of us?' Bridie Brownie removed her floppy brown hat to reveal her tumbling, brown curls.

'No, I was trying to cheer ye's up,' quipped Patsy.

Ronan dug Patsy in the ribs before he could say anything else.

'Our friend, Eamon the Elf, speaks very highly of the Brownies. 'He says you're good friends of Witch Whitely's,' he added charmingly.

'We'd hoped you could tell us where she stays in Dingle. We believe she could solve the mystery of the Merrow.'

'Of course, we're all concerned about the Merrow's safety. Witch Whitely stays at the *Blink and You'll Miss It Inn.* If she's not there she'll be in the *Crazy Horse Bar,* next door, or in *the Fairy Enclosure* at the races. I wish you luck' cooed Bridie, who was fluttering her long, brown eyelashes.

'Doh, why do they all go ga ga over that eejit?' Patsy scratched his head.

'Do they? I hadn't noticed,' said Tia, vanishing in a huff.

Chapter 3
Billy's Visitor

Billy jumped at the impatient 'rat-a-tat-tat' on the window. Pulling up the blind, he gasped at the grotesque face flattened against the pane.

'It's me, ya eejit, let me in,' said Patsy, hopping around the window ledge.

'Patsy!' cried Billy, over the moon to see his old friend.

'We've been so busy settling back into the meadow. Ye should see it, it's better than ever.' Taking off his hat, the Leprechaun climbed through the window.

'Have you found the Merrow yet?' asked Billy, helping him down.

'I bet that carrot-headed eejit has blabbed about the Unspell spell, too,' Patsy was annoyed that Cornelius had beaten him to it.

Billy nodded. 'It doesn't matter. Have you found the Merrow?'

'Not yet. Why, what are ye planning?' Patsy's blue eyes were glinting with mischief.

'Nothing.' Billy shook his head.

'I promised Mum never to run away again. I don't want to make her sick with worry.'

'Sorry. Quite right, too,' said Patsy, hopping over a pistol motif on the James Bond themed rug.

'I've some good news, though,' Billy beamed.

Patsy whistled at the new James Bond wallpaper. A dark shade of grey, it was splattered with miniature 007s. 'Hooray! Spiderman's gone for good.'

'Not the wallpaper you idiot. Some real news,' Billy laughed.

'Oh, and what's that?' Patsy was swishing the new silver blinds up and down.

'Stop it! If you break them, I'll get the blame!' Billy snatched the cord. 'Mum got a letter this morning from Pop's cousin Frank, in Ireland. He's invited us to stay on Mcloughlin's Farm. I can't wait,' he blurted.

'That's grand news. Why didn't ye say so?' Patsy, danced a little jig to celebrate. 'When are ye off?'

'Next week! So, maybe I can help after all.' Billy's cheeks were flushed with excitement.

'Ummm, this is good stuff.' Patsy, took a chocolate bar from the bedside table, and popped it into his mouth.

'It won't be easy with ye're mammy watching every move,' he mumbled with his mouth full.

'It's not Mammy, it's Mum.' Billy laughed at Patsy's cheek.

Suddenly, the door flew open, and his mum breezed into the bedroom. Patsy gulped down the chocolate with fright.

'It's time to brush your teeth,' she said. 'I'm looking forward to our holiday, aren't you?' she asked, glancing suspiciously around the room. Then kissing Billy, on the forehead, she breezed out again, without waiting for an answer.

'You should've seen your face,' laughed Billy, pulling on his pyjamas. Yawning, Patsy stretched his arms above his head.

'No, you don't get to sleep yet. I've got too many questions.' Patsy yawned again; he'd forgotten how much Billy loved asking questions.

'How does my gran send those postcards from Peru?' he asked, switching off the lamp.

'It's simple, you can send anything from anywhere in the world using the fairy post,' Patsy licked his sticky fingers.

'Are Ronan and Tia married yet?' Billy giggled.

'No, they hardly speak to each other,' Patsy hopped on to the bed.

'But why not?' Billy was alarmed.

'Don't know, Tia can be terribly frosty ye know,' he shrugged.

'Maybe you're imagining it. Mum says I imagine lots of things,' said Billy.

'No, I don't think so. It's been going on for a long time now,' shrugged Patsy.

'I told Mum that fairies live in the garden. That's why she's taking me away on holiday – she thinks I'm mad,' he giggled.

'I thought she was giving ye some odd looks. Now ye know how ye're poor gran felt.'

'Is Beltenor still angry with Ronan?'

Patsy stuck his nose in the air, and mimicking the water witch, he daintily waved his hand.

'I never want to see that ungrateful, rusty eejit again,' he sang in a high-pitched voice, just like her. Billy stifled his giggles with the pillow.

'What about Finbar and the Rat Boys?' he mumbled into the pillowcase.

'Haven't seen as much as a rat's tail since ye left.'

'Wow, maybe they won't bother the Meadowers again.' Billy stretched out on the bed.

'Wait, I haven't told ye about Witch Whitely yet,' said Patsy, suddenly remembering.

'Who?' asked Billy, shooting bolt upright again.

At last! thought Patsy, something Cornelius hasn't blabbed about.

'Witch Whitely reads the flames to find out all kinds of things. She could solve the mystery of the missing Merrow.' Patsy bounced up and down on to the bed.

'Wow, why wasn't she around when we were searching for the Healing Well?' Billy bounced up and down too.

'We're off to Kerry, tomorrow. She's at the Dingle Races,' puffed Patsy.

'She sounds a bit weird, wish I coming too,' puffed Billy.

'Billy, what's going on up there? The ceiling's falling through,' his Mum called from downstairs.

'Sorry Mum, I'm playing a game with Patsy the Leprechaun. He's come all this way from Ireland.'

Patsy couldn't believe his ears.

'Don't worry, she thinks I'm crazy,' Billy giggled.

'Don't be so silly, there are no such things as Leprechauns!' Billy's mum called back.

'What? That hurt,' spluttered Patsy.

'Go to sleep, it's getting late.'

'Sorry, Mum,' Billy called, as they dived under the duvet to smother their hysterical laughter .

Chapter 4
The Merrow

For the first time in almost a year, Finbar, the chief Rat Boy, scuttled outside in the moonlight. Bitten by a winged Imp during the battle with the Meadowers, it had taken him a long time to recover. Now well again, he watched the Palace lights dancing on the lake below and recalled the conversation the Rat Boys had overheard last night. So, snooty Queen Erin had discovered that the Merrow had an Unspell Spell that could send her home. He scrubbed his whiskers, a smirk spreading over his pointed features. What luck! All he had to do now was get to the Merrow first.

The next day, ears pricked up, and listening out for the haunting cry of the Merrow, Finbar, and his army of Rat Boys swam across the Irish Sea. Slithering from the icy water, they sniffed around the pebbly beach, their wet tails trailing over the rocks. Then spying the Merrow combing her blue-black hair in the early morning sun, they scuttled silently upwards, and threw a net around her.

The Merrow thrashed around and screeched in fear.

'Shut her up,' Finbar barked furiously. 'Queenie and the half-wits mustn't know what's happened to her yet.'

'Look,' Duke pointed out a small vessel chugging across the horizon.

'That'll be another fisherman searching for his bride. He's lucky we saved him from the Merrow's wrath. Bring her to the caves,' rasped Finbar, scurrying back into the waves.

The Merrow was tethered by the neck to a long chain attached to the cell wall.

'What do you want with me?' she wailed, while slithering around the ground.

'Give me the Unspell spell, and you're free to go.' Finbar was keeping a safe distance from her.

'Never!! The Merman gave it to me. It's to protect me from the fishermen, who'd steal my cloak, and make me their wife. Just one sip of the spell will return me to the sea!' the Merrow cried.

'Then you'll stay in chains until you change your mind,' Finbar barked.

'What do you want with it?' she hissed.

'We'd like to stop it from falling into the wrong hands,' growled Nimrev, giving the chain a vicious tug. The Merrow lunged angrily at him, the unravelling chain stopping her inches from his throat.

'You fool, Nimrev, she almost swallowed you,' rasped Finbar. The chain rattled over the floor, and eyes like stones, the hissing Merrow lunged at him again.

Afraid for their lives, Finbar and Nimrev scuttled along the tunnel. The screeches of the Merrow following them.

The next day the Merrow's alabaster skin was a deathly shade of grey.

'You're killing me,' she wailed.

'Eat, Merrow,' demanded Finbar, as a scraggy Rat Boy scampered over to place a bucket of fish beside her.

'If I die, you'll never find the Unspell spell,' she hissed.

'If you die, Merrow, my problems are over. It's your choice. No one is going to hear your temper tantrums up here,' he rasped.

She flipped her fish tail weakly, and opened her mouth to screech, but sadly, she found her voice had grown too weak.

The following day, her once shiny blue-black hair was hanging limply around her haggard face, and a terrible rasping sound was coming from her throat. Sighing pathetically, she reached inside her gown.

'Take it, and let me go before it's too late,' she whispered, handing Finbar, a bottle of bright yellow liquid.

'Certainly,' he rasped, his greedy claw closing around it. Then, laughing, out loud, he whipped the red cloak from around her shoulders. The Rat Boys guarding the cell were surprised to see a strange fairy woman cowering in the Merrow's place.

'Get away from me, you nasty rats,' she screamed, backing into the corner.

'Don't worry, she won't remember a thing,' sneered Finbar, and with a click of his fingers, she disappeared.

The fairy woman on the cliff top looked out to sea and wondered how she'd got there. Curiously, an invisible barrier was keeping her from climbing down. Wondering what she should do, she settled on a boulder and watched a huge, galleon ship, its sails billowing and Irish flag flying, gliding towards the green land.

'What's that shrieking above the wind?' Scruffy Tom cupped a hand behind his ear.

''Tis a gull,' said Dick, looking up at several squawking birds.

'Gulls don't call out "Cooo eeeeeee",' laughed Scruffy Tom.

'Look there,' said, Dick, pointing out the flock flying around the mast.

'Sounds like a gal to me,' grunted Captain Nealy.

'That's what I said, a gull,' said Dick.

'Not a gull you idiot! *A gal! Gee, ay, ell,*' he spelled, staring through his telescope. 'Shame it's not the Merrow,' he said, spotting the fairy woman waving frantically, with her blue-black hair blowing around her shoulders.

'Whoever she is though, she looks like she's in trouble.'

Dropping anchor, they scrambled down the rope ladder, and climbing into a boat, they rowed ashore.

'Coooo eeeeeee,' the fairy woman called, seeing the pirates weaving upwards, one behind the other, like a colourful dragon.

'Here, let me help you down missy,' panted the Captain, reaching her first.

'No, wait, please.' She tried to stop the Captain coming any closer. 'Ooops, too late,' she said, as he bashed his head on the invisible barrier.

'Who put that there?' he rubbed his sore head. 'There's no need to shout at me. I don't even know my name,' she howled, tears rolling down her cheeks.

'Now, now, missy, I'm no good wif water-works. I talk very loudly, that's all,' said the Captain, wishing they'd never clapped eyes on her.

'Let's start at the beginning, shall we?' Scruffy Tom felt sorry for the pretty fairy woman.

'I don't remember anything' she sobbed, louder than before.

'Now, missy, try harder,' barked the Captain.

'It's no good, it's all a blank.' She blew her nose on a handkerchief. 'Wait, I do remember.' She suddenly stopped crying. 'A drooling, ugly rat captured me, and took away my cloak.'

'A rat?' The Captain bashed his head on the invisible barrier again.

'Yes. A big, fat rat with disgusting breath, sharp, yellow teeth, and a long, black tail, who strutted around on his hind legs. That's all I can remember,' she sniffed.

'That's more than enough. I think we've found the Merrow. The question is, lads, what's that fleabag, Finbar up to now?' the Captain, asked the crew.

Chapter 5
Witch Whitely

'Are we there yet?' Tia was so excited—she'd never been away from Glendalough before.

'Yep, there's the race course below.' Ronan pointed out an oval space in the pretty scenery.

'Are we going to the races now Erin?' Tia ignored Ronan.

'No, it's far too early. We'll find the *Blink and You'll Miss It Inn*,' said Erin, feeling sorry for Ronan.

The Rainbow Bird swooped through cotton wool cloud after cotton wool cloud.

'Great timing,' cried Patsy, waving from the ground.

'Patsy, where've you been?' they called, as the bird swooped over his head. He waited for the Rainbow Bird to land, and fold away her wings.

'Across the water to see Billy,' he said.

'Why didn't you say so? Erin fluttered from the warmth of the Rainbow Bird's feathers.

'I didn't want to upset ye,' said Patsy.

'How are they?' she asked, eager for news of her family.

'They're very well. Caitlin's not too impressed with ye gallivanting around Peru, though,' he chuckled.

'I'm so homesick. What if I can't go home again?' Erin wiped the glittery tears that were sliding down her cheeks.

'I'll say ye ran off with a Peruvian millionaire,' quipped Patsy, but Erin didn't smile.

'I know what'll cheer ye up. Billy and his mammy have been invited to stay on McLoughlin's Farm. They're coming next week,' he announced.

'That's the best news!' Erin, hugged Patsy so tightly he could barely breathe.

'His mammy is bringing him to Ireland for a break because she thinks he's cuckoo.'

Erin looked puzzled.

'Billy told her that little fairies live in the garden,' he explained.

'Oh no, now Caitlin thinks we're both crazy,' Erin giggled.

'It's thanks to the Healing Well that Caitlin's well enough to travel,' Patsy reminded her.

'Yes, and I'm very grateful,' Erin smiled at last.

'Billy's keen to find the Merrow. He wants his gran home more than anything. It'll be hard with his mammy around,' sighed Patsy.

'You're right', Erin rolled her eyes. 'Caitlin will be watching him like a hawk.'

'Did ye know Cornelius blabbed to Billy, about the Unspell spell?' Patsy was still annoyed he'd beaten him to it. 'He likes to let William know what's going on. You're just jealous of their friendship,' Erin teased.

'No, I'm not. Cornelius is a terrible busybody,' Patsy scowled.

'It's right there,' insisted a Pixie in a red and white tunic, who was directing them to the *Blink and You'll Miss It Inn.*

'Where?' asked Erin, staring at an unremarkable brick wall.

'Right there,' he insisted again.

'That's a plain brick wall,' she said, confused.

'Look closer. You'll see an eye-shaped door with a shiny brass knocker.' Erin stared and stared but the wall remained a wall.

'Och, it's disappeared again, someone must've blinked. It's called the *Blink and You'll Miss It Inn* for a reason,' the Pixie tutted.

'Ye're kidding me, there's no door,' said Patsy, his startling blue eyes boring into the bricks.

'Doh, you just can't help some folk,' the Pixie muttered, stomping away.

Ronan concentrated very hard, and was pleased when the black, eye-shaped door, with a shiny brass knocker appeared.

'Oh no, who blinked?' he snapped accusingly when it vanished just as quick. Then taking a deep breath, and waking very slowly with his eyes wide open, he walked right through the wall.

'Oh no, where did he go?' gasped Erin, who was following, and then she vanished too!

Ushering Tia to the spot from where they'd both disappeared, Patsy watched her float daintily to the wall, and melt right into the bricks. He wasn't sure though if she'd found the Inn, or not. After all, it was nothing new for Tia to disappear.

'Come on Patsy, we haven't got all day. Witch Whitely will be going to the races soon.' Patsy heard their muffled voices calling from behind the wall. So, with his eyes wide open, he walked slowly through the wall, and found himself in a dimly-lit hallway with the others.

'Ahem.' Erin tried to attract the attention of a smelly, brown goat who was slumped in a comfy chair with his hooves up on the counter.

'Room WW,' he yawned, pointing a hoof at the spiral staircase without looking up.

'You haven't even asked who we're looking for yet,' said Erin, annoyed with his lack of manners.

'You're a stranger, and strangers are always looking for Witch Whitely,' he grunted.

'I've never met a friendly goat yet,' Erin grumbled, heading for the stairs.

Despite its grim interior, the *'Blink and You'll Miss It Inn'* was buzzing with fairies rushing up and down the spiral staircase. Patsy admired the green-sequinned suits, dickie bow ties, and shiny, green shoes of the leprechauns as they dashed by.

'New for this season,' said, one of them, cheekily, tipping his sparkling, bowler hat. Gnomes and

Pixies, in silver tuxedos, silver top hats, and twirling a silver tipped cane, squeezed by them on the stairs. Then came a rush of flower fairies, the golden thread of their midnight blue gowns shimmering in the candlelight.

'Wish I'd worn something classier,' Patsy whistled, even though, he'd only one suit to his name.

Standing back they let more fabulously dressed fairies rush along the corridor, and then Erin knocked on a red door with the initials *WW* carved in black.

'Who is it?' cackled a voice from inside.

'We'd like to ask your advice, Witch Whitely,' Erin called through the door.

'Every year it's the same. Doesn't anyone have any patience anymore?'

'I'm sorry,' Erin, apologised to the hook-nosed figure wrapped in a purple dressing gown, who was standing in the doorway. 'Yes, we're sorry to disturb you, but we thought you'd like to know that the Merrow is missing,' Ronan explained.

'Well, Curly, nothing's more important than the races,' she wagged a twisted finger in his face.

'The next race is in half an hour, so if you need my help, you'd better come in and help me, to choose a hat,' the Witch's, multi-coloured rollers bounced up and down in her hair.

Inside, a large spotted toad, was leaping across a red velvet draped bed, from one dusty hat box to another.

'Catch, Grimbleweed,' cackled the witch, and unravelling the rollers, she tossed them one by one. Croaking loudly, the toad caught them in its wide mouth, and popped them into a vanity case, marked with a pink *WW*.

'What about this?' She popped a pointed, blue hat on to her still, dead-straight, salt and pepper hair.

'No,' she said, seeing their eyes widen, at the sight of a hissing serpent slithering around its rim.

'This one then,' she said, swapping the serpent hat for a flapping, bat-winged creation.

'A little too wild,' said Erin, dodging the flapping wings as the witch turned around.

'Er, what colour's ye're outfit Witch Whitely?' Patsy raised his hand.

'Are you serious?' Ronan couldn't believe his ears.

'It's a blue and grey feathered number,' said the witch, and opening her dressing gown she revealed the outfit underneath.

'Crumbs!' gasped Tia.

'What's wrong?' snapped the witch.

'Crumbs, it's beautiful,' lied Tia, thinking she looked like a demented bird.

'The bat-winged hat is far too fussy for your beautiful outfit,' advised Patsy.

Ronan's jaw dropped wide open.

'What's up, Curly, you look like you're catching flies,' cackled Witch Whitely, squashing the hat, its wings still flapping, into the box. Erin and Tia giggled into their hands.

'Patsy has no fashion sense at all. This hat is perfect for your outfit.' Ronan snatched up a black feathered hat, complete with a nest of squawking black birds in the centre.

'I was about to suggest that hat,' sulked Patsy.

'Here, Broom Broom,' called Witch Whitely, and admiring the hat in the mirror, she grabbed the broom as it whizzed across the room. Then snatching up a black bag, also marked with her initials, she headed for the door.

Several winged horses in the *Crazy Horse Bar* were waiting on fairies, all beautifully dressed for the races. Passing the corny slogans on the wall like *GET A TROT ON, THE MANE MEAL,* and *THE GALLOPING GOURMET*, they followed Witch Whitely to a table.

'Five Jockey Jollops,' ordered the witch from a dappled grey horse, and in a flash, the tumblers of amber liquid had appeared.

'Drink up dear, you're paler than water,' the witch ordered Tia. Not wanting to appear rude they all drank the gurgling drinks down at once. Steam gushed from their ears, and cackling loudly, the witch tipped light blue powder onto the table and struck a match. Blue smoke swirled around the table. 'There's a stormy-eyed, fairy woman on a cliff top, who doesn't know her name, or how she got there,' she whispered.

'Never mind the stormy eyed woman, what about the Merrow?' Steam gushed from Patsy's nose making him go crossed eyed.

'Shhh.' The witch's watery brown eyes stared at him across the table.

'Someone has taken her cloak.'

'What, she must be the Merrow! Where is she?' Erin's eyes were stinging from the potent drink.

'She sits watching, high above the sea.' The witch moved her gnarled fingers over the dancing flames.

'What's she watching?' asked Patsy. 'Ssssh' the witch hissed again.

'I see a band of colourful pirates too.'

'Captain Nealy must've found the Merrow?' cried Tia, hardly able to believe it.

'Who's taken her cloak?' Ronan moved closer to the royal blue flames.

Witch Whitely raised her hands, and the flames danced higher.

'A Rat Boy, who wears his own cloak of red,' she whispered.

'Oh no it's Finbar! We should've known,' Erin gasped.

'What does he want with the Merrow's cloak?' Patsy was puzzled.

'He wants her to forget that he's taken the Unspell Spell,' she cackled, while blowing out the flames.

Chapter 6
McLoughlin's Farm

Billy smiled at the tall man with a familiar face, who was unfolding himself from the driver's seat.

'Hi,' said Billy, shocked by how much the grey-haired man with twinkling blue eyes reminded him of his pops.

'I'm Frank.' The slightly stooped giant shook his hand. 'The farm's not far. Hope you'll enjoy your stay,' he said, throwing the bags in the boot.

Billy felt a warm glow as they wound upwards, through familiar roads with the dark, purple mountains, towering on either side.

'Hope you're hungry, the missus has cooked a meal fit for a king.' Frank's eyes, twinkled like sapphires in the driver's mirror.

'I'm starving,' said Billy, who was excited at the thought of seeing Erin again. Patsy had said they hadn't seen a single Rat Boy since he'd gone home. Maybe he'd never have to see Finbar again.

Finally, the car turned right, and crunching over the gravel driveway, it stopped outside the white door of a modern bungalow with neat blinds at every window. Nothing like the farm-house that gran had described in her stories. A red-faced man was shooing sheep up the steep hill, and several horses were grazing in the field next door.

'They say you can see fairies dancing in that field at dawn.' Frank pointed over the road.

'Wicked, will I see the Leprechauns too?' Billy teased his mum.

'Don't start him off about fairies and Leprechauns. His gran has filled his head with far too much nonsense,' his mum laughed nervously.

'What? Maybe he's a chip off the old block? Your grandfather swore he saw fairies dancing as a wee lad.' Frank, clapped Billy on the back.

Frank's wife Mary opened the front door, and wrapping her chubby arms around Billy, she nearly squeezed him to death.

'Oh, he's a true Mclaughlin, just look at those ears. You must be Caitlin.' She hugged Billy's mum too. 'You're very pretty. Just like your mammy in her wedding photo.' She blew her nose on a man-size handkerchief.

'Mum, what's wrong with my ears?' asked Billy, following them inside.

Billy's room at the back of the bungalow overlooked the field. Perfect for sneaking out at night, he thought. Quickly unpacking, he rushed to the kitchen to join the adults for supper. 'The old farmhouse was falling down around our ears. The kitchen's all that remains of the original house. Your pops ate his meals in here too. Tis, a pity he never brought his new bride to Ireland. We'd loved to have met her,' Mary's eyes were filling up again.

'Gran might visit when she's finished gallivanting around in Peru.' Billy, tried cheering her up.

'That'd be lovely.' Mary plonked her round figure beside him.

'Your letter was a great surprise,' said Frank, helping himself to buttered potatoes, sliced ham and peas.

'It's a shame Billy's gran is still holidaying in Peru.'

'Yes,' his mum said frostily, hoping Frank wouldn't ask which part of Peru she was holidaying in.

'Well, as long as she's enjoying herself,' said Mary, sensing it was a sore subject.

That night, Billy was dreaming about his gran as soon as his head touched the pillow who, wearing her half-moon specs, and fluttering her silvery wings, was flying out of his reach.

A familiar voice cut into his dream and he stirred. Now, someone was calling his name. Sitting up, he parted the blinds and was surprised to see Captain Nealy, his head cocked to one side, grinning through the window.

'Captain, what are you doing here?' Billy opened the window to let him in.

'Saw ya arriving, Billy boy.' The Captain pinged his eyepatch.

'I was looking for Erin, when yourself and your mammy climbed out of big, black jalopy. Glad to see the Healing Well did the trick,' he gave a low, sweeping bow.

'All thanks to your map, Captain.' Billy saluted him.

'So, why are you here? Didn't we frighten you enough the last time?' he chuckled.

'I've come to help my gran, er, Erin. The Merrow's gone missing with the Unspell spell and gran needs to come home.'

The Captain's bushy, black, eyebrows knitted into a frown.

'I haven't a clue what you're blabbing on about. I know where to find the Merrow though.'

'What? But that's brilliant. How!' gasped Billy.

'I came across a strange fairy woman on a cliff top, who doesn't know her name, or how she got there,' the Captain explained.

'What's she got to do with the Merrow?' Billy was confused.

'The fairy woman suddenly remembered that a big, fat rat had stolen her cloak.' The Captain rubbed his long, black beard.

Billy, felt a chill run down his spine.

'Oh, no, not Finbar! So, that's why you think she's the Merrow.'

'Of course she's the Merrow, and I bet Finbar knows Erin is looking for her.' Why else would he capture her?' The Captain shrugged.

'Wait, wouldn't the Merrow be human without her cloak?' asked Billy, suddenly remembering another of his gran's stories.

'Only if a human stole her cloak in the first place, and we all know that Finbar's no fisherman,' the Captain explained.

'Erin's gone to the Dingle races with the others. They're hoping Witch Whitely will help them find the Merrow,' Billy explained.

'A witch at the Dingle Races?' The Captain was amused. 'Could've saved them a trip.'

'I'm going tomorrow with Frank. I'll find Erin and explain about the Merrow.' Billy, couldn't believe they'd found her already.

'Good boy, and be sure to tell her to hurry. The fairy woman's non-stop blubbing is driving me nuts,' said the Captain, ducking out the window.

Billy had begged for permission to go to the races. Mary had pleaded with his mum too.

'Ah, let the little lad enjoy himself. Molly, Frank's sister, lives just outside Dingle. They could stay overnight; we'll ring her later. We could have a mooch around the village. There's a book shop, and a café that makes homemade cakes.'

'Please, Mum, I've never been to the races before,' he'd whined over and over, until he'd finally got his way. Now, barely awake at six o'clock in the morning, propped up in the passenger seat he wondered if he'd dreamt the Captain's visit last night.

After a long drive through countryside and the quaint villages, Frank stopped the car outside a café/lounge bar.

'Well, young fella, I fancy a full Irish,' he said, opening the car door.

'A full Irish what?' Billy wasn't sure what he meant.

'A full Irish breakfast, you dope,' Frank laughed.

'Ooooo! Yes, please.' Billy could smell eggs and bacon wafting around the car park. Inside the café, the race goers in their fancy outfits were chatting over breakfast. Feeling hungry, Billy sat a table and waited for Frank to order.

'Psssst!'

'What was that?' He looked around. Was he hearing things?

'Psssst!' There it was again.

'Over here' hissed the small, impatient, voice.

'So, I wasn't dreaming.' Billy wasn't too pleased to see the Captain, grinning from the centre of the table.

'The rabble can put up with the fairy woman's whinging. I fancied a day at the races with my old mate Billy,' he winked, mischievously

'Please don't embarrass me,' begged Billy, watching Frank's lanky frame in a crumpled grey suit, striding back to the table.

'Well, little man, a full Irish is on the way. Don't worry I'll polish off what you can't. My auld belly thinks my throat's been cut,' said Frank, arranging the knives and forks.

'Good man, Frank.' The Captain tore off a corner of the paper napkin and tucked it down his shirt.

'Shhhhh,' Billy hissed at him.

Frank stared at the napkin, and then glanced over his shoulder.

'Who are you shushing?'

'Shushing? Who, me? I was day-dreaming. It happens a lot, ask Mum.' Billy was glad to see the waiter arriving with the piping hot breakfast.

Amused by Billy's discomfort, the Captain bent down to sniff the delicious breakfast, and burnt his nose on the red-hot plate.

'Yarghhhhhhh,' he yelped, plunging his face, into a glass of water. Frank's mouth dropped open, as the water splashed over the table. Grabbing a napkin, the Captain bent down to mop it up. Yarghhhhhhh,' he yelped, burning his backside on the other plate, and hopping up and down, he knocked over the gloopy, brown sauce. What a nightmare, thought Billy, desperately trying to clean up the mess.

'How did that happen. You didn't move a muscle. Are you a magician?' mumbled Frank, his mouth crammed with black pudding.

A floppy, brown dog trotted over, its chocolate brown eyes fixed on their table. Worried the dog had sensed the Captain, Billy wriggled uncomfortably in his seat. Sitting down, the dog growled, its sharp teeth showing under a wrinkled muzzle. Then jumping up and down, it barked loudly. The Captain flew across the table and swiping a rasher from Frank's plate, he whirled it around, and let it fly. Catching the juicy bacon in its jaws, the dog trotted off wagging its tail. Frank was completely stunned.

'Did- did you see the rasher fly off my plate and whirl around like a flying saucer?'

'You must've stabbed it with your fork,' Billy was starting to sweat.

'No, 'twasn't me. You're a magician.' Frank laughed so much he spat eggs and bacon in Billy's face.

Thankful the awkward breakfast was over, Billy was relieved to be back in the car.

The sun was shining, and it was very warm.

'Not far now, magician' said Frank, driving along the winding, coastal road.

'It's brilliant.' Billy, loved watching the giant, foamy waves that crashed onto the rocks, and hurtled sea spray into the air. Letting the window down, he enjoyed the salty smell, and whoosh of wind in his face.

'Hang on there, I'm being blown around like a piece of paper!' The Captain was clinging to the dashboard with the wind whistling around him. Tutting, Billy pressed the button, and slid the window up again. The Captain was spoiling his fun. Breakfast was a nightmare, and what else would he complain about? So far, it was Frank's driving, the cold, air conditioning, and the radio, which was too loud.

'The giant is swerving all over the place' he moaned, grasping his red, feather-trimmed hat.

'He can't help that. It's the roads; they're very narrow and twisty,' Billy glared at the Captain.

'Aye,' agreed Frank, glancing worriedly at Billy. 'The roads are very narrow and twisty.'

'Think I'll get some fresh air after all,' sighed Billy, and hitting the button, he slid the window down again.

'Billeeeeeeeee!' cried the Captain, whizzing by with his hat in his hand. Billy made a grab for him, but the wind sucked him out the window, and blew him down the road.

It was the funniest thing Billy had ever seen.

'Now you're worrying me,' said Frank, as Billy held his belly, and howled with laughter.

'Sorry, I was thinking about the flying rasher,' he spluttered, the tears stinging his eyes.

'Some very strange things happen with you around.' Frank winked.

'Well, well, here's two fine men to take a lonely widow to the races.' Molly's round face lit up like a sunbeam as she opened the yellow, cottage door.

'God bless him, he's the image of our Shane,' she sobbed, squeezing Billy tight.

Inside the cosy cottage, there were dark-beamed ceilings, an open fireplace, and flowery, winged furniture that filled the small, front room. Billy stared at a black, monstrous thing, making strange noises in the corner of the kitchen.

'It's an old-fashioned range. It heats the water, too,' said Molly. At the top of the creaky, narrow stairs, she showed him a tiny room with never-ending views over the hills.

'This is your room for the night,' she said, her eyes filling up with tears again.

'Now, don't go upsetting the child with your wailing' said Frank, prizing her arms from Billy.

'Molly was like a sister to your pops,' he explained.

Billy was worried that he always made his Irish family cry.

'Is it like seeing a ghost?' he asked Molly.

'He's a gas! And a magician too. You'll love him,' Frank roared.

Chapter 7
The Dingle Races

Hundreds of fairies milled around on the last day of the Dingle races, hoping to win the "Best Dressed" prize. There were beautiful fairies, with tiaras that twinkled in their silky hair, who'd had their wings dyed to match their flowing gowns. Elves and Pixies who paraded around, in their most vivid, colourful, tunics. Leprechauns who looked dashing in green, sequined hats, and suits, and hardworking Claurichauns, who'd swapped their leather aprons for ritzy, black tuxedos.

Music blared from the marquees at the far end of the enclosure, and under the red-striped awnings, the stalls offered butterfly cakes, candied berries, muffins, and cups of fairy wine. Shady, bug-eyed fairies in dark glasses paced outside the bright yellow flutter huts, crying *'Last chance to place your bets here!'* and acrobats, jugglers, and magicians entertained the crowd, with tricks and eye goggling illusions.

Completely unaware of the fairy folk sharing their day. The ladies in fancy hats, and gentlemen in smart suits,

sipped Champagne while inspecting the horses in the paddock. Then with their Jockeys bouncing up and down in the saddles, their boots in high stirrups, and knees tucked under their chins, the horses, gently cantered to the starting line. Finally, with a 'pop', they were off!!
 'COME ON THE WHITE HORSE!!'
 'MINE HAS ONLY THREE LEGS!'
 'GIVE HIM THE REINS!' roared the crowd. Whips thrashing, mud flying, and hooves tearing up the turf, the jockeys jostled each other for first place. The roars of the crowd, carrying them to the finishing line in a flurry of colour. At the end of the race, cameras clicked, winners cheered, and the losers tossed their betting slips to the wind. Then, with a cheery wave from the Jockeys, the horses were trotted away, to receive a rosette, or a well-earned drink.

'I've won, I've won!' Tia rushed off to collect her winnings.
 'Be quick!' Patsy pointed out the Rainbow Bird fluttering from the sky to collect them.
 'Oh, no, that's all I needed,' groaned Ronan, watching the Captain pushing his way impatiently through the crowd.
 'Captain, what are you doing here?' Erin rushed to greet him.
 'Looking for that little devil, Billy,' the Captain was out of breath.
 'William's staying at McLoughlin's Farm.' Erin was surprised.

'Yeah, but today he's at the races with the giant. I would've been too, if he hadn't opened the jalopy window.'

'Giant? What giant?' Erin giggled.

'The big fella who lives on the farm.'

'Oh, you mean Frank.' She dragged the Captain from under a sharp, stiletto heel.

'Captain Nealy, what are you doing here?' Tia hugged him, her giggle pitter-pattering in his ear.

'The Captain says William's here today.' Erin was almost bursting with excitement.

'That's wonderful,' cried Tia, who was very fond of Billy.

'Good to see you again.' Ronan offered the Captain his hand.

The disgruntled Captain turned away.

'Well, ye were never the best of friends,' Patsy laughed.

Billy was watching the leprechauns looping arms, and swinging each other around in time to the music. A cluster of flower fairies were giggling in the corner, and two pixies were trying to wake up their sleeping friend. Slurping his red lemonade through a helter-skelter straw, he wondered if anyone else could see them. He wondered about the Captain too. Even though it was hilarious, he hadn't meant him to fly out the window like that.

'Are you okay Billy?' Molly was wondering why he was grinning like a Cheshire cat.

'The magician is always day-dreaming' Frank winked. Surprised to see Patsy hovering in the doorway with the others, Billy slid off his stool, and landed with a bump.

'Sorry, I'll wash it off,' he said, pointing out a red lemonade stain on his tee-shirt. Then, jumping up, he disappeared into the crowd before they could stop him.

'William, I don't believe it. The Captain told us you were here today. I've missed you so much,' Erin fluttered to meet him.

'I've missed you too, Gran,' croaked Billy, almost in tears. 'The Captain—is he okay?' he asked, pulling himself together.

'He's a little shaken, but he's in good spirits,' Erin smiled.

'He is?' Billy was surprised.

'You've grown since last year.' Pushing his way to the front, Ronan looked up at him.

'You haven't grown at all,' Billy joked, thinking how odd Ronan looked without his armour, and that his voice didn't suit his black, curly hair.

'Welcome back,' Tia, pecked Billy, on the cheek.

'I'm black and blue, thanks to you.' The Captain shook his fist and struggled past the dancing leprechauns, who were having a whale of a time.

'Sorry, Captain,' Billy stifled a giggle. 'I tried to grab you.'

'Well, you didn't try hard enough. Luckily, a shrub broke my fall.' He patted his behind and winced.

'Billy, what are you up to?' Frank loomed over them.

'I went outside to dry my tee-shirt, but the lemonade stain won't come out,' he lied.

'What's so interesting about the floor?' Frank stared unknowingly at Erin, Patsy, Ronan and the Captain.

'Oh, I thought I'd dropped something.' Billy was trying not to laugh at Patsy, who was dancing a little jig.

'You seem a little hot under the collar. Sure, you're all right?' asked Frank.

'I'm fine. We're not going home yet, are we?'

'Nope, the last race is in thirty minutes. We'd better get a move on though. Or are you going to stand here, staring at the floor all day?'

'Okay, I'm coming. Ask the Captain, about the Merrow,' he whispered to Erin, while following Frank to the door.

'It's okay, we know about the Merrow too' she said, blowing him a kiss.

'Wait, don't you want to know how I got here!' the Captain ran after Billy.

'Not now, Captain, later,' he said, out of the corner of his mouth.

'It was terrible! I was on board a long, metal jalopy that was packed with giants, who were singing and swigging from cans.'

'You were on a coach trip,' Billy wanted to laugh out loud.

'Are you talking to yourself, Billy?' asked Molly, who never missed a trick.

'No, I was er, singing. I like singing. I sing an awful lot,' stammered Billy.

'That boy is a dreamer just like his grandfather at that age,' sighed Molly.

'Watch out Captain!' Billy, nudged him with his foot, saving him from being crushed under someone's huge leather sole.

'Watch out Captain? What did you say?' Frank was puzzled.

'Err, erm, 'Watch Out Captain!' it's the name of the horse running in the next race,' stammered, Billy.

'Never heard of it! Your day-dreaming is getting worse,' Frank laughed, and ruffled

Billy's hair.

Chapter 8
The Fairy Woman

Scuttling through the long grass, the Rat Boys spied as the Ghost ship glided down the lake. Raising their binoculars, they saw the Rainbow Bird carrying several passengers in the sky, and behind, a beaky-nosed witch was zooming, haphazardly, on a broomstick. Adjusting the focus, Finbar watched the pirates lowering the ship's anchor into the lake.

'If they want the Merrow, they can have her. She's useless without her cloak,' he rasped, his black, beady eyes now watching the Captain and the crew coming down the gang plank.

'This could be very interesting' he chuckled, tossing the binoculars aside, and then beckoning for the scraggy Rat Boys to follow him, he scurried down the hill.

'Maybe she's lost.' Standing on his tiptoes, Patsy was looking out of the palace window. 'She was right behind us. Besides, witches don't get lost,' said Tia.'

'William's grown so much, hasn't he?' Erin was so happy to have her grandson close to her in Ireland.

Ronan laughed. 'It was great fun seeing him tying himself up in knots, while lying to the big man, and his sister.'

'Poor William, everyone thinks he's mad,' sighed Erin.

Suddenly, an almighty crash made them rush outside. A pair of skinny, black-stockinged legs, in black pointed boots were sticking out of the hedge. Grabbing the kicking ankles, they gave them a tug.

'A most peculiar place to put a tree,' grumbled Witch Whitely, emerging from the foliage. 'You should've warned me Grimbleweed. You know my eyesight is poor,' she scolded the toad. The toad gave a loud croak, and with its huge eyes bulging, it vanished into thin air.

'It's no good sulking' she tutted.

'Are you okay?' Erin was trying not to laugh.

'Yes, yes, it's nothing a Jockey Jollop won't cure,' she said, brushing the prickly thorns from her black gown.

'Fairy wine might do the trick,' smiled Erin.

'Well, just a cup to calm my nerves,' she said, grabbing her bag, and barging right through them.

'If you ask me she's already had one Jockey Jollop too many,' said Patsy, making Tia giggle.

Finbar roared with laughter. Seeing the witch plunge from the sky had made his day. Queen Erin planned to find the Merrow with the help of a tipsy witch, and an ugly toad? Still laughing, he scurried into the heathery hills, with the amused Rat Boys hurrying after him. Then leaving the scraggy army to swarm inside the cave, he scuttled to the top of the hill to check on the Merrow.

The fairy woman screamed as Finbar scampered over the rocks, towards her. Alarmed, the pirates drew their swords and swivelled around.

'Put down your weapons, or I'll have the Rat Boys tear you to shreds,' Finbar rasped.

'Not before we've sent some heads rolling down the hill. Starting with yours.' Scruffy Tom pointed his sword at his throat. Finbar's whiskers twitched nervously. Why hadn't he stayed on the other side of the wall?

'I've come to set the fairy woman free. There's no need for weapons,' he grimaced.

'Why's she a prisoner in the first place?' scowled Dick, a yellow haired pirate.

'It was necessary to prevent the Unspell spell from falling into the wrong hands.' Finbar flicked his long, black tail, from side to side.

'The Unspell spell!! You mean, this fairy woman, is the Merrow. How is she to protect the fairy folk without her red cloak?' Dick stepped closer.

'Maybe, now that you're such goody goodies, you should protect them' Finbar mocked. 'Now enough of these questions, I said the fairy woman's free to go. Now, take her or leave her.'

'We'll take her cloak too' Scruffy Tom insisted.

'Don't push your luck. I've only to squeak, and hundreds of Rat Boys will be here in a flash,' Finbar warned him again.

'The fairy folk won't like what you've done.' Scruffy Tom lowered his sword.

'I'm quaking in my boots. Now, are you taking her or not?'

'How's she meant to get down; there's an invisible wall around her?' Ralph, a swarthy skinned pirate in a purple bandana, moved towards Finbar.

'Well, answer him?' How's she to get down? Do you expect her to walk through the wall?' Scruffy Tom stepped in front of Ralph.

'The invisible wall was built by a long-ago wizard. It was meant to keep out the Rat Boys,' Finbar smirked. 'She'll go through the secret gap into the cave. Follow me, I'll show you the way.'

'It's a trap! The cave's full of Rat Boys. If we step inside, we won't get out again,' Scruffy Tom raised his sword.

'Then leave without her.' Finbar scuttled over the rocks.

'Wait!' cried Scruffy Tom, putting his sword away, and following Finbar.

'Meet me on the shore by the boats.'

'Never, if one goes, we all go,' cried Ralph.

'If one goes, we all go,' chanted the pirates.

# Chapter 9

Shocking news!

Billy was dying to know what was going on. Why hadn't they been in touch, and why couldn't he find a single Meadower when he needed one. He'd tried reading a book, but all he could think about was the missing Merrow. Shocked to see a Witch zoom across the sky on a broomstick, he ran to the bedroom window. How exciting! It must be Witch Whitely, Patsy said she might help.

Dipping up and down, the broomstick, almost sputtered to a halt. Then zig, zagging all over the place it slammed into a tree, plunging the witch into the meadow.

Tearing out the front door, Billy raced across the field, ducked into the bushes, and slid down the bank on his backside. Wriggling through the tiny gap, he searched the prickly bracken, prodding it with a stick, and clambered through the thick foliage. Disheartened, he ran through the wild grass, calling out her name but still, there was no sign of the witch.

The grasses on the far side of the meadow started swaying, and Billy froze as dozens of Rat Boys, scampered along the well-trodden path. Ducking down, and hardly daring to breath, he watched as Finbar, unmistakable, in his crimson cloak, came scuttling ever nearer. Then diving into the thick, shrubbery, he rolled into a ball, and prayed he'd go away.

Billy's heart hammered at the sound of the Rat Boys, pattering around him. Stopping close to his hiding place, Finbar raised on to his hind legs, and sniffed the Meadow. Then, dropping down, he looked slowly, around. Billy, started sweating, sure, he was about to be found out. Then Finbar, suddenly, changed direction, and scampering away, he led the Rat Boys into the heathery hills. Forgetting about the witch, Billy wriggled through the gap, and scrambling up the bank, he tore across the field without looking back.

'Why did you charge outside like an elephant?' his mum was waiting when he appeared, red-faced and breathless in the lane.

'A butterfly,' he blurted out.

'Must've been some butterfly. I thought you'd seen the fairies dancing in the field,' Frank looked at him oddly. Billy wanted to kick himself, for giving such a stupid answer.

'A butterfly?' his mum repeated suspiciously.

'Yes, a fascinating butterfly,' Billy was getting quite carried away.

'What was so fascinating about it?' She felt his forehead.

'It was blue.' Billy squirmed. 'An unusual blue.'

'Ah, that'll be a Holly Blue. I'm an expert on the butterflies around these hills. Remind me to take you out on a nature ramble one day,' said Frank.

'Just my luck,' mumbled Billy.

'What was that?' asked Frank.

'Er, what good luck.' Billy gave him a cheery thumbs-up.

Billy was worried; he still hadn't heard from Patsy. He packed a torch and a bottle of water in his rucksack, and as soon as they were in bed, he opened the bedroom window. He had to find out what was going on.

'Watch out! I was just about to lob a stone at ye're window,' whispered Patsy.

'What?' Billy looked down to see Patsy, clutching a massive stone in his hand.

'You'd have woken up the whole place if you'd thrown that.'

'The pirates are missing.' He dropped the stone and dusted his hands.

Billy jumped down.

'I bet Finbar has something to do with it. I saw him, snooping around the meadow earlier. Was that Witch Whitely who fell off her broomstick?' he glanced around nervously.

Patsy chuckled. 'Yeah, she dropped like a sack of spuds, and landed in the bushes.'

'Is she okay?' Billy giggled into his hands.

'Aye, she's sleeping like a baby after drinking some fairy wine. So much for helping us out, eh?' Patsy tutted.

'Where are we going now?' asked Billy.

'Ronan says we're to search the caves for the pirates. Ye don't have to come,' Patsy shrugged, seeing the fear in Billy's eyes.

'I'm fine,' Billy lied.

'Good—this way then,' said Patsy, hopping through a gap at the side of the driveway.

Turning off the curly road that wound into the hills, they followed the moon's silvery pathway to the mouth of the cave.

'Whatttt businessss doooo youuuu haveeee hereeee?' wailed a ghostly figure, as they got nearer.

Patsy, and Billy staggered backwards with fright.

'Ye nearly gave us a heart attack,' snapped Patsy, realising it was Ronan, playing a stupid prank.

Seeing they were not amused, Ronan decided to get on with the job.

'Billy, I want you to stay here, and watch out for the Rat Boys. Give us a warning of three hoots, if you see them coming up the hill. Patsy, Tia, and Captain Nealy, you come with me' he ordered.

Before Ronan could change his mind, Billy scarpered over the rocks, and with his fingers pointing like an imaginary gun, he dropped out of sight.

Patsy had wanted to stay outside too. It was cold and dark, inside the creepy cave, and every sound made his nerves jangle. Noticing a bright light at the end of a winding tunnel, Ronan halted them with his hand.

'I heard something, coming from down there,' he whispered, leading the way.

'Why are ye wearing that armour again? 'Tis a wonder ye can hear anything under ye're tin helmet,' Patsy, trod carefully over the Rat's nests.

Ronan, gently tapped the battered, silver helmet. 'It could save my life,' he grinned.

At the end of the tunnel they stepped into a wide grotto. Water was running down the rock face, and the flaming torches on the walls, made flickering shadows in the curve of the roof.

'Look!' Erin pointed out the gagged, and bound pirates, struggling to break free on the other side of the grotto.

Suddenly, three warning hoots came from outside— but the Rat Boys were already swarming into the cave.

'This way,' whispered Ronan, disappearing into the darkness of the cave.

Finbar scurried over the rock face, the loose rocks tumbling under his claws. Sneering, he dropped a half-gnawed bone at the Pirates' feet, and wiped the grease from his wiry whiskers.

'It's no good struggling, those ropes are pulled good and tight,' he rasped, his black eyes wandering around the cave. The squeals of the Rat Boys echoed around them, then sneering at Scruffy Tom's muffled efforts to speak Finbar turned and scampered away.

Ronan waited for the last of the squealing rats to criss cross, over the rocks, and vanish into the darkness. Then drawing his sword, he ran swiftly across the cave.

'Where's the Merrow?' he whispered, hacking the ropes that bound the pirates.

'I don't know. Try over there,' a grateful Scruffy Tom rubbed his rope-burned wrists.

Ronan, pointed out the cage, and drawing his sword, the Captain, sliced through lock. The fairy woman started to scream. 'Shhhhhh, I'm not a rat,' he hissed, helping her out.

'How do we get out of here now?' Patsy's heart was hammering. 'The nests are bulging with rats.'

'We'll go around them.' Ronan was heading towards the silvery moon that hovered like a beacon in the entrance.

'Thought I smelled a Meadower or two!' Finbar's voice, suddenly boomed through the darkness. Shocked, and unsure which way to turn, they stopped in their tracks.

'Say something,' his voice mocked them.

'What do you want with the pirates?' Erin's voice shook.

'They were bait to catch the bigger fish. Besides, the dim wits walked right into the cave,' Finbar leapt to the ground, his beady, black eyes glinting in the moonlight.

'What about the Merrow?' Erin inched away.

'You can take the Merrow, but the Unspell spell, stays with me,' he rasped. Ronan's eyes scanned the cave looking for a way out. But wherever he looked, there were scores of scraggy rats crawling over the rocks.

'Why take the Merrow's cloak from her?' Ronan asked.

'Why not take it. Without it she's powerless?' he smirked.

'What do you want with us. I presume we're the bigger fish?' Erin was dreading his answer.

'You presume correct Queenie. I wanted to share some important information with you.' His pitch-black eyes wandered over each of their faces in turn.

'What information! Spit it out, fleabag,' snapped the Captain, fed up of his games.

'Gratitude, please. I want to inform you of a traitor amongst you,' he smirked.

Ronan suddenly dropped to the ground, and began rolling over and over in the dust. Then springing to his feet, he pressed his sword to Finbar's throat. Stepping from the shadows, Duke, Finbar's second in command, drew back his fist, and punched Ronan on the nose.

'Bravo, Duke.' Finbar snatched Ronan's sword, as he clattered to the ground. 'Can you guess who the traitor might be?' he laughed, enjoying every second.

Ronan tried staggering to his feet but Duke pushed him back down.

'Leave him alone,' cried Tia, rushing to Ronan's side.

'You're very loyal my dear Tree Spirit. Have you ever wondered why your hero wears such hideous armour?' Finbar, raised an eyebrow.

'That armour could save his life,' quipped Patsy, expecting Ronan to laugh.

'Maybe, he should've pulled down the face guard,' Duke smirked at the sight of the blood streaming from Ronan's nose.

'Well, Ronan? You must have something to say?' growled Finbar.

'Wait, Finbar, please spare them this. I'll do anything you ask,' Ronan begged.

Confused, Erin exchanged looks with Patsy. Surely, Ronan was playing a trick.

Finbar, leapt to the rock above them. 'This is your last chance. Your friends deserve to know the truth,' he rasped, his stinking breath swirling around the cave like rotten eggs.

But still, Ronan stayed silent.

'What the great Ronan is struggling to say, is that he wears his armour to disguise himself from those who might know him better—as the *Dark Man!*' Finbar chuckled wickedly.

'Noooooooo!' cried Billy, who'd crept inside to find out what was going on.

'Billy, the boy, where did you come from? Must be a terrible shock. At least, now you know it's dangerous to hang out with him,' Finbar wheezed with delight.

The Captain and the pirates muttered amongst themselves.

'He can't be the Dark Man, he saved my life.' Billy, was suddenly terrified by Ronan's silence.

Tia, Patsy and Erin, stared at Ronan, willing him to talk.

'Well, Ronan, or whoever you are these days. They're waiting for your denial,' Finbar sneered.

'Please, forgive me Billy,' whispered, Ronan, without looking up.

Chapter 10
Who is Ronan?

Billy lost control of his legs, and crashing through the bracken, he fell flat on his face. Blood seeped through his trousers from a gash on his knee, and biting his lip he tried not to cry. Sliding to the bottom of the steep bank in front of him, he scrambled to his feet, and ran as fast as he could.

'Billy, stop! My leprechaun leaps can't keep up with your long legs,' cried Patsy, chasing after him.

'Go away, Patsy. I don't want to talk about it. I hate Ronan,' Billy yelled.

'Ye can't go home. Ye're in shock. Ye're mammy will know something's wrong,' Patsy pleaded.

'For the last time, it's *Mum*.' Slowing down at last, he flopped to the ground. Relieved, Patsy, sat down to catch his breath.

'I'm sorry,' said Billy, lobbing a stone across the road.

'Do you remember when the Red-Haired Man, led the winged, black horse into the Forest of Darkness?' asked Patsy. Billy shook his head and frowned.

'The horse kicked and whinnied as soon as she saw him. I thought it was odd but…'

'Of course—she must've recognised him. She knew he was the Dark Man.' Billy's green eyes widened in the twilight.

'The Captain and Finbar thought they'd met him before too,' Patsy pointed out.

'No wonder he wore that stupid armour. Hope he disappears under the sea forever,' raged Billy.

'Look, the Forest Guardians are guiding Erin down the hill.' Patsy, pointed out the blue lights of the Guardians' wings, flitting in the darkness.

'Billy, thank goodness. I was so worried about you.' Erin's wings were buzzing, and her eyes were full of concern.

'Did Ronan say anything at all?' Billy was hoping it was a terrible mistake.

'No,' he didn't even answer when I called his name,' Erin shrugged.

'I can't believe Ronan is the Dark Man. I missed him so much. What'll happen now? Where will he go?' asked Billy.

'I don't know, and I don't care,' Patsy was in shock too.

'I trusted him with my grandson,' Erin shuddered.

'Where's Tia?' Billy suddenly missed her. 'Why was she so unfriendly towards Ronan? Has she known his secret all this time?'

'No, Tia didn't know anything,' said Patsy, hoping he was right.

The spindly legged, Forest Guardians flitted off to guide the Captain and the pirates down the hill.

'I'm surprised Finbar didn't stop us leaving the cave.' Patsy was watching the Guardians' magical, blue wings flitting up the hill.

'Finbar will be laughing his ugly head off. He's finished Ronan, and taken the Unspell spell. He knows I can't leave without it.' Erin was feeling utterly defeated.

'Ronan's vanished into thin air. There must be another way out of the cave,' said Scruffy Tom, joining them.

'I knew there was something dodgy about him, but the Dark Man? Just as well he didn't stick around.' The Captain, whose face was blue from the light of the Guardians' fluttering wings, swished his sword in the air.

Patsy noticed the sun rising over the hill. 'It's almost daylight, they'll be up soon on the farm' he told Billy.

'I want to talk to Tia first,' Billy, paced up and down shaking his head.

Erin touched his cheek. She hated seeing him so upset.

'You can speak to her later. Patsy's right, you should go home now.'

'Yeah, and take the fairy woman with you,' said the wily Captain, trying to get rid of her.

'The fairy woman can stay in the oak tree for as long as she likes,' said Tia, suddenly appearing beside them.

'Tia!' Billy gasped. 'Did you know that Ronan was the Dark Man?'

'Of course not. My heart's broken,' she sobbed.

'But you were frosty with him?' said Patsy.

'I wasn't frosty' she blubbed into her handkerchief.

'Those withering looks almost turned him to stone,' Patsy insisted.

'I thought he was the Stranger. I was upset that he hadn't been honest with us.'

Erin put a comforting arm around Tia's shoulder.

'Why the Stranger though?' Billy was puzzled.

'I heard the Stranger's speech the day he chased the Rat Boys from the meadow. He said *"he'd returned the Meadow to King Marty, and the Meadowers."* Ronan, used the same words the day Billy went home. It was like hearing the Stranger's voice all over again. When I asked him about it, he didn't deny it.'

'He can't be the Dark Man, and the Stranger,' Billy was more confused than ever.

'Only Ronan knows the truth, and now he's gone,' Tia, wiped her eyes.

Suddenly, there was a swirling breeze from Witch Whitely's broomstick as she swept over them.

'That's a much better landing than the last time,' Patsy grinned as she climbed off her broomstick.

'You must be Billy. Why such a long face? Did something happen while I was sleeping?' She turned her back on Patsy.

'We found out that our friend, Ronan, is the Dark Man.' Billy still found it hard to believe.

'What! The handsome, curly-haired chap? Can't be! You liked him too, didn't you, Grimbleweed?' The toad hopped onto her hand with a loud croak.

'Who told you that he's the Dark Man?'

'Finbar the Rat boy, and now Ronan's disappeared, so it must be true,' said Billy, sadly.

'Well let's see what the flames say about that' she said, tipping yellow powder on to the ground.

'Stand back' she warned, striking a match and throwing it in.

'*Flames reveal to me… the Dark Man's true identity*' she cried. Thick, black smoke swirled around them making them cough, and huddling anxiously around the flames they waited for an answer.

'Well that is odd the flames have gone out.' she said, looking at a burnt, smouldering patch, on the ground. Erin, was beginning to wonder if the witch would be any use at all.

'That's a nasty cut,' she said, noticing blood on the knee of Billy's trousers. 'Grimbleweed,' the witch, clicked her fingers, and with a slurp, the toad's long tongue shot out and licked the blood stain away.

'That tickled' giggled Billy, rolling up his trouser leg to examine his knee. 'Thanks, Grimbleweed' he gasped, amazed there wasn't even a single scratch.

'Now, to find the Merrow, the keeper of the Unspell spell' announced Witch Whitely, pleased something had worked at last.

'You're too late, the pirates rescued me. That beast still has my cloak and my Unspell spell though' the fairy woman raised her hand.

'Ah, yes, you're the Merrow. I saw you in the flames,' the witch remembered. The fairy woman frowned, wondering what she was talking about.

'So, we've to find the cloak, and the Unspell spell?' Witch Whitely tried again.

'Yes,' they nodded, wondering why they'd invited her along.

'Well, we are in a pickle, aren't we? Let's see what the flames can tell us,' she cackled.

Chapter 11

Ronan's Big Mistake

So, Ronan's friends had discovered the truth, and his little adventure was over. Beltenor's eyes were whirling like Catherine wheels, and changing every colour of the sea. Now that he was back, she was going to make him pay for leaving in the first place.

Looking around the cold, bleak, Quivering Palace, Ronan remembered how he'd met Beltenor on a deserted Brittas Bay beach, all those years ago. The beautiful water witch had crashed through the waves, giving him a fright. Slowing his winged, black horse to a trot, he'd stared fascinated by her, and by the golden-haired, water Nymphs that followed her around, feeding her shrimps, arranging her gown, combing her hair, and attending to her every whim. Then with its great jaws snapping, a ferocious Sea Malion had emerged from the sea, and lunged at Beltenor, as she lay basking in the sun. Galloping to her rescue, Ronan had drawn his sword, and sliced off the sea monster's head.

Her eyes had whirled a deep, sea blue as she'd thanked him.

'I owe you my life, Ronan.' she'd said.

'How do you know my name,' he'd asked, climbing off his horse.

'Everyone knows who you are now. The water nymphs discovered that while you were locked away, the Dark Man committed many crimes.'

Ronan looked puzzled.

'Finbar disguised himself as the Dark Man, to terrify the fairy folk of the valleys, and to lure the children of the villages to the caves. Those who heard his haunting cry, believe it was the Dark Man.' Ronan felt sick. Finbar had destroyed his reputation, while he'd been locked away in the Castle.

'A poster declaring *"Prince Ronan of the Mound in Galway"* to be the Dark Man was nailed to every tree in the valley. Now, all but the Meadowers who, were living under the ground, fear you.' Ronan, was shocked, how was he to prove his innocence?

'I need a strong guardian to protect me. The urchins do their best but the truth is the Malions swallow them by the hundreds. No one will bother you in the Quivering Palace,' she'd trilled, in her musical way. With no other choice, Ronan, had reluctantly accepted her offer.

'Are you listening? I said there'll be no monthly jaunts to the beach. I don't care about the problems of the Meadowers. Look where my generosity got me the last time,' Beltenor's shrill voice jolted Ronan back to reality. He should've known it was a mistake to come back. This time, it seemed she intended to keep him a prisoner. The monthly trips were all that had kept him sane the last time.

'Now, fetch those useless Water Nymphs. It's time for my massage' she trilled, her eyes whirling like dark, ocean pools. Resisting the urge to tell the cantankerous water witch to fetch them herself, Ronan, clanked miserably down the quivering stairs. Several, of the golden-haired nymphs flitted to her immediate attention, and sitting forlornly on the steps, he wondered what he'd done.

He'd thought about seeking out the help of the Red-Haired Man but was afraid he wouldn't believe him. Tia was so angry with him, he couldn't possibly have told her the truth. So, with no other choice, he'd found himself back inside the Quivering Palace. Time dragged by in the cold, gloomy, underwater world, and the days were even longer than he remembered. What was he thinking? He'd hated being Beltenor's skivvy the first time around. 'Fetch this, fetch that. Do this, do that,' her demands were never-ending. The Water Nymphs drove him mad too, forever combing her hair, painting her nails, plumping her cushions, and feeding her all day long! Nothing could brighten up this humdrum existence.

He missed the sunshine, and imagined the warmth of the rays, that pierced the grey sea on his face. He missed the smell of the grass after a heavy rainfall, and the leaves rustling in the breeze. He missed the wild flowers in the meadow, and the animals grazing in the fields. He missed breathing in the fresh air. Most of all though, he missed his good friends. Beltenor would only permit him beyond the Palace walls, to slay the Sea Malions, the human-headed fish, that were the scourge of the sea. She'd warned him that the sea urchins would clap him in irons if he tried to leave. Somehow, he had to get the urchins on his side. He hadn't willingly committed any crimes. It was time to stop being ashamed and fight for his reputation. Whatever must Billy think of him?

Chapter 12
The Cloak and the Unspell Spell

Billy, couldn't believe that when Finbar had shrunk him last year, he'd actually fitted through the tiny front door of the oak tree. Now, thankfully a normal size boy again, he could just about squeeze through the side door.

Sitting quietly, they waited for Witch Whitely, to rummage through her bag. At last, scattering yellow powder over the floor, she threw in a match.

'The Unspell spell, dangles on a chain around Finbar's neck' she said, staring into the golden flames.

'No way, urghhhhhh, I don't want anything that's been hanging around that smelly rat's neck.' The fairy woman, looked totally disgusted.

'The Unspell, spell is my only chance of going home,' Erin, was amused that the fairy woman was so terribly timid, and fussy. Whereas the Merrow would've ripped the spell from around Finbar's scraggy neck.

Tia poured them each a peculiar, green drink, from a tall jug. Sipping it, Billy wrinkled his nose.

'Can you see the Merrow's cloak yet?' asked Patsy.

'There's a dome-shaped shack inside the cave.' They gathered around the hazy images, and Witch Whitely moved her gnarled fingers over the flames.

'Look, it's Finbar's nest, and there's the cloak hanging behind the door,' Billy cried.

Erin was so excited, her eyes filled with tears.

'I don't know how to thank you, Witch Whitely,' she said, amazed that the witch had proved useful after all. 'Now we know exactly where to find the cloak and the spell.'

The witch was quite relieved. After all, she hadn't got off to the best of starts.

'Don't thank me until we have them safely back where they belong,' she smiled.

'I'll need the Merrow's permission to use the Unspell spell. So, the fairy woman must have the cloak first.'

'Hang on! What if the Merrow doesn't let you have the spell?' Patsy raised an eyebrow.

'I would never refuse permission,' snapped the fairy woman, offended by his remarks.

'Please, use the Unspell spell first,' urged Patsy.

'The Merrow will allow you to return home once she knows the full story,' insisted fairy woman.

'As soon as the cloak's around your shoulders, you'll change your mind,' Patsy disagreed.

'The Merrow does have a terrible temper. She could fly into a rage,' agreed Tia, topping up their drinks.

85

'You too, Tia? Doesn't anyone have a good word to say about the Merrow?' the fairy woman sighed.

'Not really,' said Patsy.

'That's not true, the Merrow gave me the chance to become human even though it disgusted her. I married, and had a beautiful daughter because of her, and now I have my wonderful grandson. I'll always be grateful to the Merrow for her kindness, and generosity,' said Erin.

'Ummm, this drink is very tasty, even though it smells like grass,' said Billy, who wasn't paying the slightest bit of attention. They laughed, and Patsy rolled his eyes.

'The Tree Spirits love it too, it was made fresh this morning,' gushed Tia, pleased he liked it.

'The Merrow is very powerful, and without Ronan, we may need her help. I still think it's better to let the fairy woman have the cloak first,' Erin pointed out.

'What do ye think, Patsy?' asked Witch Whitely.

'I like to gamble but even I wouldn't care to bet on this one. There's a slim chance the fairy woman will remember her promise. She remembered the big, fat rat, didn't she?' she cackled.

'I'm not sure I want the cloak. The Merrow, sounds truly awful,' grumbled the fairy woman.

'Well, if we're finished, I'll whizz off, and see what's going on.' Witch Whitely blew out the flames.

'Don't worry I'll let you know when the coast's clear' she called, as her broomstick swirled over the trees.

Billy was sleeping soundly when he was woken by a loud thud. Opening the window, he looked down at Patsy.

'You almost broke the glass you idiot,' he hissed, still half asleep.

'We've to get a move on.' Patsy was stomping around impatiently. 'Witch whitely says the Rat Boys are sleeping.' Excited, Billy jumped down, and pulling on a blue hoody, he followed him through the hedge.

The decaying food lying around in the rubbish-strewn tunnels made their stomachs heave, and every step they took inside the cave was matched by the drip, dripping of water. Rounding a bend, they were taken by surprise by a swaying light, whizzing towards them.

'It's a dimwit Bally Bog, and he's heading straight for us.' The Captain jumped backwards.

'Has he seen us?' asked Billy.

'No, but he will, if we don't shift. Get down,' he barked .

Scrambling into a crevice, they watched the strange Bally Bog, a lantern swaying in his hand, and its googly eyes rolling in its sockets go zooming by. Behind him, propelling itself along on stumpy legs, was a flame-throwing Shingle Dragon, snapping at his heels.

Patsy, shook with laughter, 'that's made my day,' he roared. Be careful though, there could be more Shingle Dragons around,' he warned.

Dodging in and out of the recesses of the cave they avoided the scurrying Rat Boys. Then crawling the length of a dingy tunnel, they spied Finbar's nest up ahead. A dim light glowed in the murky window, and the makeshift door was slightly ajar.

'We'll watch out for rats and the Shingle, er, thingys,' whispered Witch Whitely, who was hovering with Tia in the background.

'The cloak's still behind the door,' Billy peered through the filthy window.

'I could squeeze in there,' said the Captain, determined that, after yet another tearful tantrum that morning, he'd reunite the fairy woman with her cloak. Wrapping Scruffy Tom's bandana around his face to block out the dreadful smell, he bravely, squeezed inside.

It was dark, except for the faintest glow of a lamp, inside the nest. The Captain, reached for the cloak, and then froze, when out of the corner of his eye, he saw the faint, orange glow was moving around. Then suddenly, a Shingle Dragon sprang from the darkness, and with flames flicking from its nostrils, it pinned him to the ground.

Afraid for the Captain's life, the pirates barged through the door, and awoken by the commotion, the Rat Boys swarmed down the tunnel.

The Rat Boys surrounded them, and dragging the Captain from under the Shingle Dragon, Finbar shoved him outside. 'Drop it, or the Shingle Dragons will have your friends for supper,' he ordered, seeing a rock clenched in Billy's fist.

Billy glanced at the dozens of Shingle Dragons slithering from the darkness, and realising it was hopeless, he dropped the rock at his foot.

'No doubt the wispy Tree Spirit and the flaky witch will be back.' Leaping to the rock above them, Finbar scampered up the rock face, until he was eye level with

Billy. Then whipping off his cloak he waved it like a matador tormenting a bull.

Billy's head spun so fast, he thought he was going to be sick. Grabbing the rocks he tried to steady himself. Then he started tumbling at a frightening speed, with the cave whirling around him, and suddenly he stopped shrinking with a sickening thud.

'It's simpler this way. Now get them out of my sight,' roared Finbar.

Chapter 13
Where's Billy?

Billy wasn't in his room! Thank goodness his mammy had left early to spend the day in Dublin with Mary. Hurrying down the lane, Frank called out his name, but there was no sign of him. Maybe, he was in the village spending the pocket money he'd collected from his relations over the weekend. It was Saturday morning, and the village wasn't far away. Maybe, he knew that he'd been up all night, tending to a sick cow. Of course, that was it, Billy hadn't wanted to disturb him.

Shop shutters were opening, and the stall holders in the busy market place, were calling out a cheery 'hello'. One by one, Frank popped into the newsagents, the book shop, the café, and the supermarket but no one had seen Billy, since yesterday. Hurrying back to the bungalow, he searched for a note, and finding nothing, he dashed out to the car.

Billy gawped through the bars of the cell, into the never-ending blackness of the cave. Finbar had taken Erin's wand, and Patsy's gold dust, and he'd separated them from the Captain and the pirates. As if that wasn't enough to worry about, fire-breathing Shingle Dragons were roaming around, and watching their every move. Where was the Rainbow Bird, when they needed her?

'Mum will have a fit if she sees me like this,' said Billy, who was now the same size as Patsy.

'We'll worry about that later. We have to get out of here first. Now, put your thinking caps on,' said Erin, trying not to panic.

'It's morning already.' Billy noticed the daylight seeping through a crack in the wall.

'Mum's going to Dublin today, she won't know I'm missing. It won't be long before Frank notices, though.'

'Frank won't want to worry your mum not unless he has too,' Erin was relieved Caitlin would be spared the horror of knowing William was missing—for a little while, anyway.

'Fingers crossed, we won't have to tell her at all,' she winked.

'I wish Ronan was here. He'd know what to do,' Billy whined.

'Well, he's not, so get used to it,' snapped Patsy.

'What if he's the Stranger, and not the Dark Man?' Billy wanted it to be true.

'So why run away, if he's so innocent?' asked Patsy.

'We could break out. We might find him in the Quivering Palace' said Billy.

'Stop it, William. You know Ronan is hiding something.' Erin was cross.

'But Gran, Ronan was your good friend.' Billy was surprised.

'Where is he now, when we need him?' Erin snapped again.

Feeling tired, Patsy took off his hat, and slumped to the ground.

'Tia, and Witch Whitely will get us out, you'll see,' he said.

'Beltenor wouldn't let us into the Palace anyway.' Billy was still thinking about Ronan. 'She blames us, for taking him away in the first place.'

'She offered to let Ronan help to find the Healing Well,' Erin reminded him. 'No one forced him to stay on dry land.'

'Beltenor says I'm very irritating. She likes you, though.' Billy tickled Patsy's beard. 'She says you're sooooooo cute,' he teased.

'Don't think I'm going into that miserable Quivering Palace. She mightn't let me out again. But she was right, ye are irritating. Now, if ye don't mind—I'll need forty winks if we're to make a plan,' said Patsy, squashing his hat over his face.

Erin laughed; she'd forgotten how they wound each other up.

'What's that?' Billy saw something tumble to the ground from Patsy's hat.

'It's a pouch of gold dust.' Patsy snatched it up and waved it around. 'It was inside my hat all the time.'

'High five.' Billy slapped his palm on Patsy's.

'High five, big ears,' said Patsy, jumping to his feet.

'Sssshhhhhh,' whispered Erin, grabbing Billy's hand.

'Sprinkle the dust before it's too late.'

'Gold dust, work fast – and free us with an almighty blast!' Patsy sprinkled the fine dust around the cell. A feeble puff followed a few weak sparks, and suddenly they were outside in broad daylight.

'Hardly the mighty blast I'd expected. I thought we'd be safely back in the meadow,' grumbled Patsy.

'Never mind, we're free, aren't we?' said Erin, spinning around in delight.

'We can't leave the Captain and the pirates here,' said Billy.

'Shhhhh, what's that?' Patsy was concerned about the scratching above them. Crouched down, and ready to pounce, a Shingle Dragon was teetering on the ledge above them. Several more were slithering behind it. Turning on their heels they fled, but leaping down, the Shingle Dragon sunk its teeth into the tail of Patsy's coat.

'Get off him,' Billy pummelled the dragon over, and over with his fists. Then bravely he tried prising open its jaws. The dragon turned on Billy, and grabbing its tail, Erin whirled it around and around, with the flames flicking dangerously around them.

'Wow, that was wicked!' cried Billy, as letting it go, she sent it flying over the edge.

'My father taught me that years ago. It's much more entertaining when they land in water with a great, big, orange splat,' she giggled. Then, grabbing their hands, she dragged them down the hill.

Flapping its vast black, wings, a swamp rat swooped around them, knocking Erin off her feet. Then grabbing Billy in its razor-sharp talons, it lifted him off the ground

Patsy punched the flapping, cawing, swamp rat, and grabbing Billy's feet, he yanked him to the ground.

'Jump,' he yelled, giving him a shove. Closing his eyes, Billy flew over a deep ledge, and landed in the road with a thud. Sailing after him, Patsy and Erin, landed on the road too.

A black car hurtled around the corner, and with its tyres smoking, it squealed to a halt. The car door flew open.

'Get in,' barked the driver, just as the Shingle Dragons slithered onto the road. Looking up, they were shocked to see it was Frank.

Chapter 14
The Plan

Ronan was bored with waiting for the Sea Malions to attack. It could be weeks before his plan was put into action at this rate. He'd even considered making a break for it while Beltenor was having yet another pampering session.

'You're very quiet, I hope you're not pining for that little flibbertigibbet?' Beltenor's eyes were whirling a deep sea-green.

'Tia is a very dear friend of mine,' said Ronan coolly, knowing who she meant.

'How dare you speak to me like that.' Beltenor's voice was flat, and her eyes were like muddy whirlpools.

'Have you forgotten that I took you in twice, when you had nowhere to go?'

'How can I forget when you remind me every second of every day? Have you forgotten how often I've saved your life?' Ronan replied angrily.

Beltenor's eyes whirled out of control, and shooting forward, she scattered the water nymphs, who were plumping her cushions.

'Get out of my sight. If you try to leave I'll have you clapped in irons,' she screamed.

Feeling oddly satisfied at having made Beltenor more hostile than before, Ronan headed down the stairs.

Suddenly, the Palace began to shake, and with a glimpse of the terrifying Sea Malion, through the transparent walls, Beltenor was thrown from her seat. Its seal-like body was slicing through the water, and its curly, black tendrils were floating around its grotesque, human face. This was Ronan's big chance. Turning back, he galloped up the stairs with his sword already drawn.

'I'll need the sea urchins help. There are two Malions outside the Palace,' he panted.

'I saw only one Malion.' Beltenor's eyes were strangely still.

'Look outside if you don't believe me.' He pointed out the pair of Malions that were circling the Palace like sharks.

'Surely, a guardian should be brave enough to fight them alone.' Beltenor narrowed her eyes, which were now a deep, sea-blue.

'Very well, then they will destroy the Palace,' said Ronan, walking away.

Another pounding from the Malions scattered Beltenor's precious gems around the floor, and almost tipped the Palace over.

'Fetch the urchins if you must,' she shrilled, her eyes spinning like Catherine wheels. Worried, she'd fly into a rage, the water nymphs quickly gathered up the gems.

Clanging up the steps two at a time Ronan rang the underwater bell. Then, swimming through the Palace roof he waited while the urchins dropped from the rocks and the sea plants.

'I'll fight the Malions alone,' he told the millions of eyes peeping from within their spiky shells.

'Why ring the bell if you're to fight the Malions alone?' Interested in what Ronan, had to say, the urchin leader was unfurling his purple prickles.

I'd like the urchins to allow me to swim to the surface,' Ronan told him.

'You'll... fight... the... Malions... alone... if... we... allow... you... to... swim... to... the... surface.' The purple leader repeated Ronan's words very slowly, so the multitude of urchins could hear.

'I won't stop him,' said a blue urchin, her spiky blue shell snapping shut.

'Suits me,' said a red-spiked urchin, burying himself in the sand.

'Absolutely,' chorused the others, and burrowing into the seabed, they disappeared.

A Sea Malion watched with its bottomless eyes, while circling around the Palace. Ronan swam closer, then suddenly, corkscrewing through the murky water, he drew his sword, and sliced off its head. Turning around, he found himself staring down a huge, pink throat. Moving suddenly, the second Malion slammed into him, making him drop his sword. Ronan watched the bubbles trickle from its nostrils, and glanced at his sword, glinting on the sea-bed below. Something shifted, and shooting out of the sand, the purple urchin leader rolled like tumbleweed across the seabed, grabbed the sword, and passed it up to Ronan. Gripping the sword in both hands, Ronan swung it with all his might. With its curly, black tendrils floating around its grey, lifeless face, the second Malion's head sank to the bottom of the sea.

Saluting the brave urchin leader, Ronan spiralled to the surface of the sea. Breaking through the waves, he gasped for air, and wearily, crawled on to Brittas Bay Beach. He'd made up his mind. He'd go to Fizard, the old wizard who lived in the Meadow. Staggering to his feet he looked out to sea, and taking off his heavy armour he hurled it into the waves.

Chapter 15
Frank's Secret

Frank, gripped the steering wheel, as he careered around the winding roads.

'How do I explain this to your mammy?' he barked at the miniature-sized Billy, who was sitting in the back seat looking very glum. 'Why didn't you think before gallivanting off in the night.'

'Finbar shrunk him, mister,' said Patsy, who was battered and bruised from the bumpy ride. Frank couldn't believe the Leprechaun had made such an obvious comment.

'Then we'd better find a way to unshrink him before his mammy goes ballistic,' he growled.

'Let's look on the bright side. We escaped,' said Patsy, trying to cheer him up.

'His mammy, won't see any bright side! All she'll see is Tom Thumb, here!' Frank jerked his thumb over his shoulder. Billy couldn't speak; not even to tell Patsy to shut up.

'It's all my fault.' Erin fluttered to the front seat. 'William was only trying to help,' she said.

'I don't care who's to blame. I only care about unshrinking Billy, before his mammy comes home on the 7.30 bus.'

'Who the hell is William anyway?' he barked, becoming slightly hysterical.

'Witch Whitely has a bag of lotions and potions. She might help,' said Erin, trying not to cry.

'At last—sounds great to me. Where do we find her?' asked Frank.

'She'll be in the Magical Meadow, in the oak tree,' said Patsy.

'Why didn't you say that you could see the fairies, too?' Billy found his voice at last.

'Ah, I wondered if you'd ever speak again,' Frank, eyed him in the mirror.

'You could see them all along, but you never said.' Billy was annoyed.

'I was enjoying seeing you trying to wriggle out of every disastrous situation. Flying rashers… classic. The gift of sight only ever got me into trouble. Nothing like your escapades, though. Creeping out in the dead of the night. What were you thinking Billy? It's so dangerous.'

'I'm sorry. It didn't feel like I was in any danger. I was with my gran,' Billy pointed to the front seat. Frank looked down at Erin, who was fluttering her silvery wings.

'Oh no. You mean, she's your gran. Your gran's a fairy? What's going on?' I thought she was gallivanting around in Peru.' He slammed on the brakes, and they shot out of their seats

'I can explain everything,' said Erin, taking a deep breath, and looking up at Frank.

'Someone better had,' he barked.

'I'm a flower fairy from the Magical Meadow, in Glendalough. The Merrow changed me into a mortal, so I could marry your cousin Shane. It's true I'm William's gran, and it's my fault we're in this mess.'

'This is a bad dream,' Frank, ran his hands through his thick, grey hair.

'When William's mammy became sick last year, he ran away to find the Healing Well in Glendalough. By following him to Ireland, I broke the Merrow's spell. Now, you see why I can't go home,' she said, fluttering her silvery wings.

'So, if you hadn't followed Billy, you'd still be his sweet, old gran,' Frank shook his head.

'Now Finbar's stolen the Unspell spell, and Gran might be a fairy forever' said Billy, sadly.

'What a mess.' Frank wondered if he should pinch himself. Maybe, it was all a bad dream.

'Now you know the truth, we'd better find Witch, Whitely. We'll be in worse trouble if his mum sees him like this' said Erin.

Still in shock, Frank opened the car door.

'This way,' said Patsy, and jumping down he disappeared through a gap.

'How many fairy gaps are there?' Billy followed him.

'Hundreds. We're never far from the Magical Meadow. That's it, Mister, wriggle on your belly,' called Patsy, through the gap.

'What do you think I'm trying to do,' panted Frank, who was stuck halfway. Trying not to laugh, Patsy gave a whistle, and before long, a gang of tittering Gnomes, Pixies, and Elves were shoving him from behind.

Free at last, Frank gawped at the vivid green and purple scenery on the other side of the hedge.

'Tis like a painting,' he sighed. Several Claurichauns in brown leather aprons began polishing his shoes.

'Sorry, fellas, we're in a hurry,' he said, shooing them away. One of the little Claurichauns grabbed Billy and whirled him around.

'You were heading for home, the last time I saw you,' cried Donal, surprised.

'Hi Donal,' cried Billy, pleased to see another old friend.

'I had to come back, Finbar's captured the Merrow, and the Captain, and the pirates. Erin, can't come home because he's stolen the Unspell spell, too.' Billy explained.

Donal was shocked. 'Surely there's something we can do? The Merrow protects us from the rabble on the sea. Besides I thought we'd seen the last of Finbar.'

''Don't worry Donal, Witch Whitely is helping us. The Meadowers have worked so hard, they're settled now. I promise to send for you, if we need you.' Erin thanked him.

'We're hoping Witch Whitley has a spell, to make me grow again,' said Billy.

'As soon you're fixed, you're coming home with me,' said Frank, wondering what on earth he'd gotten himself in too.

'That's not fair, they'll need me. Especially now Ronan's not around' Billy argued.

'Ronan, you mean your friend with the black, curly hair?' said Frank.

'Yeah? How do you know him?'

'I've seen him around. Where is he today?' Frank looked around the meadow.

Erin's green eyes were brimming with tears. 'Ronan's the Dark Man,' she said.

'I met the Dark Man, many years ago. He was galloping down the lane on a winged, black horse,' said Frank.

'Were you scared? Did he hurt you?' asked Billy.

'I was scared, because I'd heard terrible stories about him. But he scooped me on to his horse and took me home to my ma.'

'That doesn't make sense. I thought the Dark Man was evil,' said Billy.

'Later, I was told my tears had melted a curse that wicked Brianne had put on him.'

'What curse? Who's Brianne?' asked Billy.

'Brianne's a fairy sorceress who lives in the woods. It was Finbar's idea to have him cursed with a black heart. That's how he became known as the Dark Man.'

'What happened to him?' Erin had never heard this part of the story.

'He soared over the mountains on his winged, black horse, and freed the children who were imprisoned in the caves. The Rat Boys locked him away in the Black Castle. Then one day, someone left his horse grazing by the castle gates, and unlocked, the dungeon door. That day, the Dark Man escaped, and was never heard of again.' Frank was staring at the mountains.

'Do you know who unlocked the dungeon?' Billy was wide-eyed at Franks' story.

'It was me' he smiled; 'I led his horse into the forest. Then I stole the keys from the sleeping guard, and unlocked the dungeon door. It was the least I could do. After all, he'd released the children from the caves.'

'Are you the little blonde boy gran told me about. The boy who lost his voice, after seeing the Dark Man?'

'Yep, I lost my voice for four years. They thought I'd never speak again.'

'Wow,' cried Billy, who hadn't expected that. Even Erin hadn't realised who he was.

'I believe my story proves the Dark Man wasn't bad after all.' Frank winked.

'Billy was so excited. 'Do you think it's Ronan.'

'Could be, some say he was a Prince from Galway. Maybe Ronan was a Prince?' shrugged Frank, striding ahead into the Magical Meadow.

Chapter 16
Fizard

There was nothing magical about the meadow when Ronan had visited many years before. Back then, the grass was so brittle, it had crunched under his feet. The trees were bare and dotted with empty birds' nests, and the brook under the rickety bridge was as dry as a bone. Worried, Ronan had sent his horse away to find fresh grass and water, and then he'd hidden in the undergrowth to avoid the Rat Boys that constantly sniffed around the meadow. By day, he stayed under shade of the trees, and at night he listened to the chatter of Tree spirits, the practically, invisible fairies that wafted around like little ghosts. It was by listening to them, he learned that Finbar, had banished King Marty, Queen Olivia and the Meadowers to live under the ground. It was thanks to Finbar, the meadow was no longer magical. It seemed there was no escaping the Rat Boy's wickedness.

After a few nights of hiding, Ronan had stumbled across the wizard of the meadow. Huddled over a crackling fire, his wizened face was hidden under strands of long, white hair, and around his shoulders, he wore a threadbare robe. Offering Ronan a cup of hot fairy punch, he nodded to where his winged, black horse, grazed on fresh, green grass.

The next day, Fizard (so called, because he was both fairy, and wizard) spread a soothing potion on Ronan's eyes. 'To restore your sight, and give you renewed strength' he'd told him. Ronan blinked, and gazed around the meadow. It was the first time since leaving the Black Castle that he could bear the daylight. Then, with his wise grey eyes smiling, Fizard had handed him a snow-white shirt, a pair of black breeches, and a mask. 'I've been waiting for the right Prince to come along. It's time for the masked *"Stranger"* to set the Meadowers free,' he'd said.

Unlike that first visit so long ago, today, Ronan thought the meadow was truly magical. Happy to be rid of Beltenor, he noticed the birds tweeting merrily, in the silver-leaved trees. The butterflies, flitting around the swaying wild flowers. The bees, humming softly in the air, and the brook running freely under the rickety bridge. Wading through the long grass, he scanned the meadow, trying to remember the way to Fizard's camp. Climbing a tree, he saw the purple smoke of the wizard's fire curling into the clear blue sky to the west.

He found Fizard, sitting by the fire like all those years before. As if expecting Ronan, he stood up and gripped his hand.

'I have some upsetting news,' he greeted him.

'What is it?' asked Ronan.

'Finbar has captured the Captain, the crew, and the fairy woman.'

'But I saw them leave the cave.' Ronan felt guilty. Why did he run away?

'They returned to the cave for the Merrow's spell, and cloak,' Fizard explained.

'What about Tia, Billy, Patsy and Erin?'

'All unharmed, except, Finbar has shrunk the boy.' He stoked the fire with a stick.

'Finbar's told them about my past.' Ronan hung his head.

'Finbar created the Dark Man,' Fizard reminded him.

'They'll never believe that a little boy's tears made my heart good again,' Ronan sat down by the fire.

'This is not the time for feeling sorry for yourself. Your friends need you more than ever. The little boy is now a grown man, who lives on McLoughlin's Farm. He's told them the Dark Man's story. I'm sure they'll believe you now,' Fizard reassured him.

'Frank's the little boy I took home to his mammy all those years ago? He has the gift of sight too? The crafty old… just wait until Billy finds out,' Ronan burst out laughing.

'But how do you know all this? You never seem to roam far from this fire.'

'The flames tell me what I need to know. I know that you hated being Beltenor's guardian again,' the old wizard chuckled.

'That's strange, I met a witch who reads the flames too. Do you know Witch Whitely?'

'Yes, she's my sister. She taught me everything I know. Fizard Whitely, at your service.' He bowed.

Ronan, was surprised.

'Well, your sister is helping Erin to find the Unspell spell, and it looks like she's tracked it down.'

'Ah, the flames didn't offer any news of my sister,' said Fizard.

'I bet she'd love to see you again. Why don't you come with me,' Ronan, noticed that Fizard's eyes were more watery than usual.

'No, we argued many years ago. She wanted more than this,' he swept a hand around the camp. 'Selfishly, I wanted her to stay. Last I heard she was studying lotions and potions with the Brownies on the Boyne. She knows where to find me,' he added stubbornly.

His bony finger pointed into the fire.

'What is it?' asked Ronan.

'Finbar's moving your friends to the Black Castle?'

Ronan watched as the hazy images appeared in the flames. Scuttling along, and shoving the fairy woman, the Captain and the pirates in front of them, were Finbar, and the Rat Boys, scuttling towards the Forest of Darkness.

Chapter 17

The Almost Always Spell

Witch Whitely rummaged through her bag. 'It's here somewhere,' she said, tossing out the bottles of lotions and potions.

Frank crouched down to look through the tiny door of the oak tree. 'Hurry up, we've only a few hours left,' he pleaded.

'It's called the Almost Always spell, it's here somewhere, she assured him.

'Why's it called the Almost Always spell?' asked Billy.

'Because it Almost Always, works, silly,' cackled the witch.

'Sounds like it might Almost Always, not work to me,' shrugged Billy.

'Ta da,' she announced holding up a green bottle. Then with a click of her fingers, Grimbleweed, produced a pair of round specs.

'Well, it seems straightforward enough,' she read the instructions with her specs teetering on the end of her nose.

'It's really that simple?' Frank was peering through the tiny window.

'Yes, yes, very simple,' said Witch Whitely. 'You must sprinkle the feet of the afflicted—that's you, Billy—with the powder, and he'll grow like a plant, under a full moon,' she cackled, pleased with herself.

'What! When's the next full moon?' Frank was alarmed.

'Oh yes, let's see.' She flicked through a note book. 'Ah, here we are, yes, there's a big, fat, full moon, tomorrow night.'

Billy's face fell. 'What happens now?' he asked.

'That's thrown a spanner in the works,' said Frank, looking a lot calmer than he felt.

'Billy's mammy is home tonight! There must be something ye can do,' said Patsy.

'The Almost Always spell is all I have.'

'We could snatch Finbar's cloak, and try to reverse the spell. There's no guarantee it'll work, though,' Patsy suggested.

'Billy's in enough trouble,' snapped Frank, thinking it was a stupid idea.

'Sorry, only trying to help,' said Patsy, feeling quite hurt.

'What if the Almost Always spell doesn't work?' Erin was feeling panicky too.

'We'll have to leave the country. His mammy can't see him like this. Look at the state of him. He's barely the size of two tall hats,' said Frank.

Witch Whitely rolled her eyes. 'Have faith' she said, 'the spell will work.'

'We don't have any other choice. I'll phone Mary, I'll persuade her to take your mammy to the theatre. I'll suggest the last bus home tomorrow night. That'll give us time to use the spell, under the full moon,' said Frank.

'Are you going to tell Mary what's happened to me?' Billy was worried.

'No chance. She'll have the doctor hammering down the door. I'll say we're going on a fishing trip.'

'Here, Billy.' A few minutes later, Frank was holding the huge mobile phone to his ear. 'Your mammy wants to know about the fishing trip. I've spoken to Mary' he winked.

'What's that, Billy? Speak up! Your voice sounds so small and far away,' his mum yelled.

'I SAID, WE'RE HAVING A GREAT TIME. CAN'T WAIT TO GO FISHING. YES, WE'LL BE BACK LATE,' Billy hollered.

'Mum can't hear me,' he pushed the huge phone away.

'Oh, we'd better go now. Yes, I know the signal's very bad today. Bye, enjoy the theatre,' Frank, wondered again, what he'd gotten into.

'What about the fairy woman, the Captain, and the crew? We can't just leave them in that cave,' said Tia.

'Of course not, we'll go back for them, but William has to stay here with Frank.' Erin felt terribly guilty.

'Frank could come too. We should all stick together,' protested Billy.

'What do you think Patsy?' asked Erin.

'Whatever I say he'll bite my head off,' Patsy, looked sideways at Frank.

'We might as well come along. We have to wait for the full moon anyway,' Frank shrugged, to everyone's surprise.

'Good let's see what's happening inside the cave.' Witch Whitely scattered yellow powder on the ground, threw in a match, and cackled as it gave a loud puff!

Frowning, she added orange powder to the flames.

'What's up?' asked Patsy, as bright orange smoke swirled around them.

'Ah, that's much clearer. The cave is empty. Looks like Finbar's taking your friends to the Black Castle, the witch cackled.

'Why would he do that?' asked Tia, appearing in front of them.

'Finbar doesn't want you getting your hands on that spell' said the witch.

'There'll be no more creeping out at night when this is over. I'll sleep in your room if I have to,' warned Frank, worried that things were about to get worse. 'Do you hear me, Billy?'

'Yes,' nodded Billy, still gawping at the orange flames.

Chapter 18

Reunited

Hoping to reunite the old wizard with his sister, Ronan had persuaded Fizard to go with him to the Forest of Darkness. How Ronan, longed for the days, when he'd rode everywhere on his winged black horse. They'd already hidden in the undergrowth several times to avoid the sniffing, scuttling Rat Boys. Finally, making it through the Magical Meadow they'd crossed the upper lake in a leaky rowing boat, and climbed into the Glendalough hills for a much-needed rest.

The view was breath-taking. The broody purple mountains towered over them, and the upper lake sparkled like a sheet of glass below. Looking around, Ronan couldn't help remembering Billy's disappointment at discovering that St Kevin's bed was just a stone-cold slab. Not a real bed like he'd expected, complete with a pillow and blanket. He smiled, he missed Billy, Tia, and Erin and sometimes he even missed Patsy too.

He'd plucked up the courage to speak to King Marty and Queen Olivia on his way through the meadow. They were concerned; they hadn't heard from Erin since she'd left in search of the Merrow. Ronan had assured them he'd bring her home. Then, taking a deep breath he'd told them about his past. At first, they were a little afraid of him, but after hearing his story they'd relaxed. The King remembered well, how the Stranger had driven the Rat Boys back to the wetlands, and for that he said, he'd always be grateful.

To his surprise, Queen Olivia had thanked him too.

'It's thanks to you that Billy's mammy is fit and well again,' she'd said.

Ronan felt much better for getting it off his chest. He still wasn't looking forward to facing the others though.

'Look, there's the entrance to the Forest of Darkness.' Ronan pointed to where two soot-black trees stood out in the greenery.

'I'll light a fire, I have to consult the flames, if we're to plan an escape' said Fizard, climbing down the hill.

It was a chilly night, and relaxed in the warmth of a blazing fire they washed down bread and cheese with a steaming mug of nettle tea. Ronan scratched at the dirt with his sword.

'We can avoid the Truds here, here and here,' he said, marking the rough map he'd drawn with three crosses.

'Truds?' Fizard, looked puzzled.

'Yes, mud trolls that live deep in the gurgling swamps,' said Ronan.

'Swamps?' Fizard's grey eyes grew wide in the firelight.

'You can stay behind if you prefer,' said Ronan, realising Fizard wasn't that keen.

'Are you mad? You can't go to the Castle alone.' Fizard's bony finger pointed to the hazy images in the flames, and Ronan's heart sank. The Rat Boys were scurrying around the Castle grounds.

'It looks like Finbar's brought his whole army along,' he whispered.

'Ssshhhh, what was that?' Fizard heard a suspicious rustling. Peering through the bushes around their camp, they saw a figure creeping about in the dwindling twilight. Moving quickly, Ronan dived on the figure, and grappled it to the ground.

'Get off me,' puffed the mystery figure, its arms flailing in the air.

'Billy? What are you doing here?' asked Ronan, recognising his voice, and letting him go.

'We could ask ye the same question.' Patsy was helping Billy off the ground and brushing the muck from his clothes.

'Fizard, is that you?' Witch Whitely swept across the ground on her broomstick.

'Ah, my dear sister it's good to see you. I heard you were assisting these good folk,' said Fizard, almost shyly

'Sister!' cried Billy and Patsy together.

The blue wings of the Forest Guardians flashed on and off with excitement. Happy to see Fizard too, the toad croaked, loudly. Then with a flick of his long tongue, he dried up Witch Whitely's tears.

'I see Grimbleweed's as loyal as ever,' Fizard laughed.

'Ronan, where've you been?' Tia, who'd appeared from nowhere, couldn't believe her eyes.

'Wait,' Billy stopped Ronan from moving any closer.

'Are you the Dark Man, or the Stranger?' he asked.

Chapter 19

Escape from the Black Castle

The Captain peered through the bars of the cell, for the hundredth time. The light from the flaming torches high on the walls flooded the corridor. Looking down he was pleased to see the fat rat guard was sleeping at last.

'We need a piece of rope and a hook,' he pointed to the keys, sticking out from under the rat guard's cloak.

'Will this do?' The fairy woman took a pin from her hair.

'Now for something to attach it too' said the Captain gruffly.

'Twine?' asked Scruffy Tom, undoing the knot of his makeshift belt.

'No wonder they call you Scruffy Tom,' the Captain laughed.

Twisting the twine, and looping the hair pin through the end, he lowered it through the bars. 'It's got to work. No one's going find us out here,' he mumbled. The twine tickled the guard's nose, and they held their breath. Turning over, he grunted and started snoring again.

Relieved, the Captain gently hooked the key with the hair pin.

'Drat,' he whispered, as it slipped off.

Hooking it again, he slowly pulled the twine upwards. Just as the key was within their grasp, it fell to the ground with a clatter. Startled, the Rat Boy scrubbed his whiskers, and after a quick glance around, he fell asleep again.

'We'll be stuck in here for good,' wailed the fairy woman.

'For pity's sake, we're trying,' hissed the Captain.

Dick looked through the bars. The key was lying tantalisingly by the leg of the chair.

'Quick, unravel the twine. I'll reach it,' he whispered.

'It's not long enough to reach the floor,' snapped the Captain.

'Let him try,' insisted the fairy woman.

Determined, Dick unravelled the twine and lowered it anyway.

'It's too short,' he hissed, pulling the twine back through the bars.

'I told you so.' The Captain was pacing up and down.

'Look,' Dick couldn't believe his eyes. The key had lifted off the ground and was now floating upwards by itself.

The Captain pushed Dick to one side and, slipping through the bars, the key landed at their feet. Surprised, the pirates gathered around to stare at the rusty key.

'You didn't think we were going to leave you here, did you?' asked Tia, melting through the solid door like a ghost.

'Tia, how did you find us?' they asked, huddling around her.

'Witch Whitley's flames tracked you down. Quickly, we must go now. There are hundreds of Rat Boys inside the Black Castle. The Forest Guardians will light our way through the forest.' Turning the key in the lock, Tia shooed them out into the draughty corridor.

'What happened to him?' The Captain was surprised to see the guard, gagged and trussed up like a chicken.

'Oh, I forgot to mention I bumped into an old friend of ours.' Tia blew on a thin, silver whistle, and the Red-Haired Man came galloping down the corridor, the hooves of the winged, black horse clattering on the stone. Leaning down, he grabbed the fairy woman and lifted her into the saddle. Relieved, the pirates began to scramble on, too.

'Cowards! We're not leaving without the cloak, and the Unspell spell. They're in a wooden casket, somewhere within these walls,' the Captain barked at his crew.

'Don't worry about that, Captain, just get on the horse. I need you to protect the fairy woman. There's a secret passage that will take us to the cloak and the spell,' the Red-Haired Man's deep voice boomed along the corridor.

'I'd rather stay and face the rats,' said the Captain, refusing to go.

'Myself and Ronan have a plan,' the Red-Haired Man insisted.

The Captain shook his head. 'The last I heard, your friend Ronan was the Dark Man.'

'For pity's sake, Ronan's innocent. Now, get on the horse, and I'll explain on the way.' Suddenly, a black carpet swept down the corridor, and rearing on her hind legs, with her leathery wings beating wildly, the horse trampled over the Rat Boys that were swarming around her shins.

Pulling the Captain into the saddle, the Red-Haired Man cracked the reins, and with the Rat Boys sweeping after her, the winged, black horse galloped along the corridor, and soared upwards into the eaves. Then, dodging the Rat Boy's shillelaghs, she escaped through the window. Squealing with rage, the Rat Boys turned back, and sweeping along the corridor, and up the stone steps, they scampered into the Castle grounds. Soaring over them, the horse followed the blue lights of the Forest Guardians' wings into the pitch-black Forest. Listening to the angry squeals, and the pattering of the army below, they flew deep into the forest. Then suddenly, the Forest Guardians stopped and waited, their blue wings dancing in the dark. Then, with the Rat Boys almost upon them, they parted, allowing the vermin to tumble into a hidden swamp behind. A Trud rose slowly from the swamp, a Rat Boy writhing in each fist, and with mud dripping from its torso. Then bellowing into the darkness, it ducked back into the swampy depths.

'I love you, Forest Guardians,' the fairy woman cried into the darkness.

'Wicked!' called Billy, punching the air, who sitting on Witch Whircly's broomstick with the others, was circling the swamp.

Chapter 20

The Cloak and the Unspell Spell

Duke and Nimrev scampered across the castle grounds.
'What happened?' growled Finbar.

'We found a message pinned to a tree in the forest.' Duke handed him a tatty piece of paper.

They followed too closely and sank in the mud. I fear that the Rat Boys were swallowed by the Truds.

'What's the meaning of this?' Finbar screwed up the cheeky message and fired it at Duke's head.

'How does a boy and his band of idiots keep getting away with this? Gather the remaining army, and then guard the cloak and the Unspell spell with your lives,' he rasped, scurrying into the darkness.

Frank had waited outside the forest, afraid the Rat Boys would spot his towering frame. Now, listening to the excited chatter of how the Forest Guardians had tricked the Rat Boys, he wished he'd been there too.

'Maybe we could speed things up. I can help out if you like,' he said, anxious to get Billy sorted out before his mum came home.

'Sorry Frank, it's out of the question. Finbar will see you a mile off,' Fizard, warned him.

'Ah that's a shame,' said Frank. 'You see, now Billy's back safe and sound, I'm not too keen on letting him go again.'

'Perleaesssssss, please, let me go,' whined Billy.

Erin touched his arm.

'I promise he'll be safe. It means a lot,' she pleaded. Frank looked at their eager faces, and despite feeling uneasy, he nodded.

'Well you're his gran,' he said, thinking it was odd to address a tiny fairy, with silvery wings, as gran.

'I suppose I can be there in minutes. This is the very last time though,' he warned Billy.

'Thanks, you're the best, Frank,' Billy punched the air.

Patsy gave Ronan a thumbs-up. 'Your plan worked a treat,' he said.

'You were all great,' Ronan reminded him. 'It was close,' said the Red-Haired Man, still annoyed with the Captain for refusing to get on the horse.

'Yes,' agreed the fairy woman, who was fed up with the Captain bossing her around.

'The Captain likes giving the orders.'

'And why not? I am a Captain,' he barked.

'It's great having you back, Ronan,' Erin butted in, putting a stop to their bickering.

'Yep, never doubted ye for a minute,' quipped Patsy, slapping him on the back.

'Liar!' said Billy, giving Patsy a shove.

'I don't blame you for doubting me. I should've told you the truth from the start,' Ronan admitted.

'Never mind. You're back, and that's all that matters,' said Tia, giving him a hug.

'Urghhhh' shuddered Billy.

'Now, let's see where the cloak, and the spell, are hidden inside the Castle.' Gathering around the small fire, Witch Whitely moved her gnarled fingers over the flames.

'*Fire, crackle and burn well. Flames dance high, and lead us to the cloak and the Unspell spell.*' She closed her eyes for a second. Then snapping them open again, she pointed out the image of a wooden casket, glowing in the fire.

'They're inside the casket,' she whispered. The room holding the casket is here,' she pointed to an image of an ornate staircase that had appeared in the dancing flames.

'The Rat Boys don't know about the secret passage at the side of the Castle. Come on, I'll take you there.' The Red-Haired Man jumped on his horse.

'Don't worry Frank, the Forest Guardians will let you know if we need you,' Erin promised.

The horse's leathery wings beat silently up and down as she carried them over the forest. Billy glanced behind at Witch Whitely, Fizard and Grimbleweed, who were following on the broomstick, and below him, the Forest Guardians were flitting like tiny, blue stars.

At last, the turrets of the Black Castle, visible against the blacker sky, came into view. Wings slowing, the horse glided into the Castle gardens, and Billy's tummy flipped a dozen times. Following the Red-Haired Man through a hidden door at the side of the castle, they slipped into a dingy passageway. Then creeping up a flight of rickety stairs, they crossed the grand landing, and tiptoed to the top of the ornate staircase.

'Get down, there are two Rat Boys guarding the room with the casket,' Ronan whispered.

'We can't let them stop us now,' Billy tutted.

'I'll distract them, and then I'll disappear' offered Tia.

'No, ye grab the cloak and the spell,' said Patsy, and before they could stop him, he was dancing an Irish jig on the landing. The Rat Boys watched his shadow dancing on the wall, then springing from their seats, they cornered him like a mouse.

Billy's eyes popped out of his head. 'Someone help him, please!' He yelled, watching the Rat Boys creeping closer, and closer.

Stretching his arms in front of him, Fizard began chanting over and over, *'power of the woods make them still... power of the woods make them still... power of the woods, make them still.'* Then suddenly, a bolt of green lightning flashed from his fingertips, and zig zagging across the landing, it struck the Rat Boys and turned them to stone.

'Blimey!' said the old wizard, amazed.

'Well done, brother,' cried Witch Whitely, proudly.

'The Green Man of the Woods taught me that years ago. I'm amazed it still works,' he beamed.

'Patsy, what were you playing at. Fizard turned them to stone.' Billy's heart was still banging.

'Well, that's gratitude for ye,' snapped Patsy, although very grateful to Fizard.

Stealing past Duke and Nimrev, who'd both frozen in mid pounce, an ugly smirk on their face, they raced into the room to find the wooden casket, tucked away in a corner. Taking a deep breath Ronan opened the lid.

'Look, here's Erin's wand, and a full pouch of gold dust!' A delighted Patsy swiped them from the casket.

'Never mind about them.' The fairy woman's eyes were resting on the red cloak underneath.

'Here's the Unspell spell, at last' cried Erin, grabbing the tiny bottle and passing it to the fairy woman.

'I'll need the Merrow's permission before using the spell' she smiled.

'No, don't risk it. The Merrow will turn nasty' Patsy warned her again.

'Please, use the Unspell spell first.' The fairy woman, was offended by Patsy's remarks.

'No, not yet.' Billy worried that if Erin changed into his gran too soon, she wouldn't be able to keep up.

'Leave it until we're safely outside the forest. There's no time for this now,' Tia whispered impatiently.

Folding the Merrow's cloak, Ronan tucked it safely inside his shirt. Noticing Duke and Nimrev were already starting to crack, they flew down the stairs and raced along the secret passageway and out into the Castle gardens.

'Fiiiiiiiiind them!' they heard Finbar roaring into the darkness.

Realising he'd discovered the cloak and the Unspell spell were missing, Ronan, Captain Nealy and the Pirates drew their swords and charged the Rat Boys, who were barring the Castle gates.

'Take the reins!' ordered the Red-Haired Man, throwing Billy on to the horse. Then drawing his sword, he charged after them.

'Quick, Patsy, jump!' hollered Billy, seeing a Shingle Dragon creeping up behind him. Taking a long, leprechaun leap, Patsy landed safely in the saddle. Fizard was zapping the Rat Boys that were scurrying over the broomstick with the bolts of green lightning that were still shooting from his fingertips. Missing her bag of tricks, Witch Whitely was booting the Rat Boys with her pointy, black boots.

'Hold on!' called Billy cracking the reins, and flapping her mighty wings, the horse galloped to the Castle gates and soared over them into the forest.

'Golden dust, save us all from danger. Trickle down softly, and change the Dragons' fire to water.' Patsy blew gold dust from his palm, then cheered to see the water gushing from the Shingle Dragons nostrils. Then with a blinding flash of her wand, Erin froze several Rat Boys, scuttling around on the ground.

Billy tugged at the reins. 'Take us back; we're not leaving without the others,' he whispered in the horse's ear.

Another blinding flash from Erin's wand sent an attacking swamp rat crashing to the ground.

'Yah!' cried Billy, cracking the reins again.

'Look out!' cried Erin, seeing a black mass approaching them, across the sky.

Chapter 21
The Rhyme

Worried about all the screeching that seemed to be coming from the forest, Frank hurried through the trees. A cluster of blue lights were flitting across the pitch-black sky, and as they drew nearer, a tiny Forest Guardian zipped down to perch on his finger.

'Hurry!' Her wings twinkled like blue diamonds in the blackness.

'Billy's in trouble, and the Castle is crawling with Rat Boys and Shingle Dragons.'

'Quick, show me the way,' barked Frank, who was striding into the blackness.

'Wait,' a little voice piped up behind him, and turning around he was surprised to see Donal, the shoe-polishing Claurichaun they'd seen earlier in the meadow.

'Looks like we're just in time,' he said, giving a toot on a wooden whistle. The shrubbery began to shiver, and the King's Dwarf Guardians, clad in shiny, golden armour, flew into the forest with their bows and arrows at the ready. King Marty and a whole Kingdom of Meadowers followed them on foot.

'This way—please hurry,' whispered the little Forest Guardian, her wings were buzzing anxiously.

Frank was shocked! Ronan and the Red-Haired Man were fighting with Finbar and Duke. Steel clashing, and dancing around each other, they were locked in a vicious sword fight. The Captain was rolling around in a cloud of dust, swapping punches with Nimrev. Why, he wondered, had he allowed Billy to become involved in this?

The Meadowers took up their positions, and loading their catapults with heavy stones, they pelted the Shingle Dragons, who were blasting the forest with fire. The Swamp Rats were dragging the winged horse across the sky by the reins. Hearing Billy's cries above its terrified whinnying, Frank sprinted through the trees. Dropping the reins, the Swamp Rats flapped wildly around his head, biting and scratching his face.

Horrified, Witch Whitely turned the broomstick around. 'Hold on Fizard,' she called, and zooming downwards, she scattered the vicious rats, and crashed into the ground.

'Draw back your bows, and fire,' screamed Georgia, the leader of the Dwarf Guardians, seeing more Swamp Rats approaching. Gliding through the sky, the hail of arrows struck the flapping rats, sending them plunging into the forest.

'Promise you'll never come back to Ireland, Billy. My auld heart couldn't stand it.' Frank was relieved to see the winged black horse landing safely with her passengers.

Billy couldn't believe that the Rat Boys were running away.

'Where's Finbar, Duke and Nimrev?' he asked.

'We sent them scuttling into the Castle.' Ronan clapped Donal on the back.

'Sniffling cowards,' chuckled King Marty.

'That was awesome,' cried Billy, giving King Marty a 'high five.'

'I'm so proud of you, young man' the King's blue eyes twinkled.

Patsy looked around the forest.

'Did you see Witch Whitely, and Fizard, there were awesome too. They saved Frank from the rats.'

The Forest Guardians spread their wings, filling the forest with a soft, blue light.

'Look over there,' Tia, pointed to a broomstick poking from the bushes.

'Are you all right?' Patsy helped the bedraggled pair to their feet.

'Of course, we haven't that much fun in ages,' replied Witch Whitely, making them laugh.

Fizard was shocked to see the deep gauges on Frank's cheeks.

'Did the vermin do that to your face?' he asked.

'Grimbleweed!' shrilled Witch Whitely, and hopping up to a high branch, the toad flicked out his long tongue, and licked Frank's wounds away.

'Thanks, Grimbleweed, you'd be very handy to keep in the medicine cupboard.' Frank was delighted. Now he wouldn't have to explain the wounds to Mary.

Billy gave Erin a great, big, hug. 'I can't believe Finbar ran away.'

'I can't believe I allowed you to walk into a battlefield' said Frank, who was still shaken.

'I'm sorry, Frank. It got out of hand very quickly,' Erin apologised.

'You're telling me,' nodded Frank. 'I'm just relieved Billy's still in one piece.'

'Let's go before Finbar changes his mind.' Witch Whitely was swirling into the sky on her broomstick, with Fizard and Grimbleweed on board.

'Meet me at St Kevin's bed above the upper lake,' she called.

Billy and the others climbed on to the horse, and thanking King Marty and the Meadowers again, they followed Witch Whitely across the sky.

Jumping down when they reached the lake, Billy anxiously patted the horse's nose and waited for Erin to unroll the Merrow's cloak.

'The fairy woman must put the cloak on first. I'd like the Merrow's blessing to use the Unspell spell,' she said.

'Don't say I didn't warn ye,' said Patsy.

'I've made my decision' said Erin, but before she had a chance to change her mind, the fairy woman had swished the cloak around her shoulders.

'Are you a fisherman?' asked the Merrow, appearing with a loud boom, her stony eyes, staring at Frank.

'No, your Merrowship. I'm a farmer,' Frank replied.

'I shan't be your wife, do you hear me,' she screeched, almost bursting their eardrums.

'I'd say the whole of Ireland heard you. I have a wife and I assure you I have no need of another.' Frank wasn't sure whether to be amused or terrified.

'One drop of the Unspell spell will make my hair writhe with snakes, and cover my face with pimples' she hissed.

'Don't exaggerate, Frank's a farmer; he's not interested in you. You were rescued by the pirates?' The Merrow swivelled around to glare at the pirates, her fish tail, flipping agitatedly.

'You're the miserable one,' she hissed, her eyes resting on the Captain.

'Silence, how am I supposed to speak,' she screamed at Billy, Patsy, and the pirates, who were laughing at the Captain's expense.

'That's better', she said, glowering at them. 'I remember now, a rat with disgustingly bad breath captured me. Wait,' her stormy eyes sprang wide open. 'I was a snivelling, pathetic fairy woman?' she said, in disbelief.

'Do you remember promising me the Unspell spell?' Erin asked bravely.

'What?' The Merrow's eyes bored into her. 'I'd never make such a promise. You took advantage of a snivelling fairy woman' she accused. 'The Merman gave me that spell to keep me safe at sea. Who'll protect me, if I give the Unspell spell away?'

'Please, you must remember me. I'm Erin, the flower fairy. You changed me into a mortal so I could marry my true love Shane. I'm sorry that I broke the spell. I came back because my grandson was in danger.'

'You should never come back, no matter what the circumstances. What's the point of having rules if you're going to break them?' She eyed Erin, who stood trembling in her silver dress.

'I warned ye, I knew she wouldn't keep her promise,' said Patsy.

Erin put a protective arm around Billy. 'I'd do it again tomorrow to protect my grandson,' she said.

'Please Merrow, it's all my fault that she's stuck here,' Billy begged.

'Your bravery impresses me. The Merrow's tone was friendlier, and they were shocked to see a single tear run down her face. 'I'd like to show my gratitude. After all, you returned my cloak. Therefore, I shall give you the Unspell spell, if, the miserable one agrees to protect me.'

The Captain nodded. 'At least I won't have to put up with the fairy woman again,' he said.

'Wow, thank you, Merrow, you're great.' Billy danced up and down, and everyone cheered. 'Can we have the spell now?' he asked, afraid she'd change her mind.

'It's not that simple you stupid boy. This rhyme explains how to use the Unspell spell.' The Merrow fished in the pocket of her cloak and handed a scroll to Erin. Unrolling it, she read out loud:

The Merrow, it's my job to save.

If captured Merrow, drink me, to free yourself from those who'd keep you as a slave.

Be warned that no else should drink me, for I am as bitter as a poisonous thistle.

If, however, you are chosen by the Merrow, you may only drink the Unspell spell from a bottle of the rarest crystal.'

'Here,' sighed the Merrow, handing over the spell.

Silvery tears cascaded down Erin's cheeks.

'You wanted the spell, didn't you?' The Merrow was confused.

'I'm sorry William, the spell's useless. I can only drink it from a rare, crystal bottle,' Erin sobbed.

'Surely you can find a crystal bottle.' The Merrow's eyes were cold.

'But, but—' stammered Billy.

'Silence, boy!' The Merrow put her hand up.

'That'll be like looking for a needle in a haystack.' Tia was disgusted.

'Where do ye suggest we start?' Patsy was enraged.

'B, but—' Billy stammered again.

'Quiet! You have the Unspell spell and all you can do is cry,' hissed the Merrow.

'It's useless without a crystal bottle.' Ronan was disappointed too.

'Then give it back to me.' The Merrow held out her hand.

'No, no. That's what I've been trying to say. I have the crystal bottle,' Billy blurted at last.

'What? How? Where?' Asked Erin, staring into Billy's green eyes.

'Don't you remember? I filled the crystal bottle with the healing water from the well,' he cried.

'Billy, you're a genius.' Erin kissed him on the cheek. 'Where's the bottle now?'

'At the farm, in a wooden box,' said Billy, proudly.

'Silly boy—why didn't you say so?' hissed the Merrow.

'I'll meet you there.' Frank was already striding across the field. 'With a bit of luck, we'll catch the full moon, and this nightmare will be over by tonight.'

'Take the horse. She's yours, after all.' The Red-Haired Man offered Ronan the reins.

'No, you're her new master now. You've looked after her well. It'll be a pleasure to ride with you, though,' said Ronan, lifting Billy into the saddle.

Chapter 22
Race against the Moon

Frank was shocked to find that Billy's bedroom had been ransacked. His books were strewn across the carpet and his wardrobe and drawers had been emptied onto the floor. Picking up a small wooden box lying on its side, he went outside.

'What's up, is Mum okay?' asked Billy, worried by Frank's expression.

'Yes, yes, your mammy's fine. I found this' said Frank, showing him the empty box.

'Where's the crystal bottle? It was inside? No one else knew it was here,' cried Billy, who was shaking.

'Finbar's taken it, who else could it be. He's determined to stop Erin from going home.' Patsy couldn't bear the pain in Billy's face.

'Quick, we have to find him before he reaches the Black Castle.' The Red-Haired Man leapt back on to the horse.

'No, wait.' said Witch Whitely, shaking some yellow powder onto the ground and throwing in a match. Moving her bony fingers over the heat, she read the dancing, yellow flames.

'Patsy's right, Finbar's read the rhyme. Duke knew about the bottle, because he's been snooping around the farm for days.' Billy shivered. Duke must have watched him through the window. Now it made sense. 'Finbar wasn't running away. He was rushing to get to the crystal bottle first.'

'Look' Witch Whitely pointed out three hazy images in the flames.

'Finbar, Duke and Nimrev are on the road to Tinnehinch,' she whispered.

Frank, ushered them to the car.

'It'll be quicker,' he said, and with Ronan clinging to the dashboard, and Billy rolling around in the back with the others, he sped out of the driveway.

'We should be ahead of them by now' he said, parking the car in the bushes after a long run.

'Ssshh.' Witch Whitley spotted the Rat Boys; their raggedy ears, scraggy whiskers and long tails silhouetted by the golden moon behind them.

'Wait for them to come closer,' whispered the Captain. The pirates tightened their grip on the thick rope they'd hurled into a tree.

'Stay close Billy, it's nearly time to use the Almost Always spell.' Frank looked up at the moon rising in the sky. 'Your mammy will be home in an hour, and I don't want anything to go wrong.'

'Now!' ordered the Captain with a drop of his hand, and with a whoosh!! the Rat Boys were scooped up in a net, and dangling from the tree.

'Works every time.' The Captain was pleased with himself.

Finbar struggled to free his long snout from the netting. 'You'll pay for this' he growled

The Merrow slapped the net, hard, with her tail. 'Frightening, isn't it?' she hissed.

'Get off me you idiots!' Finbar rasped at Duke and Nimrev, who were trampling him in their panic.

'Come on Billy, we're running out of time!' Frank snatched up the crystal bottle, as it dropped through the net.

'I want to punish these disgusting rats for what they did.' The Merrow slapped the net with her tail, for a second time, sending it swinging into the air.

'Yeah, they'll only gnaw their way out,' agreed Billy, as the Rat Boys became more and more tangled.

'Let the Merrow deal with them. We have the crystal bottle and the Unspell spell. We have to go before the moon disappears from sight.' Grabbing Billy by the collar, Frank hurried to the car. Gathering a bundle of heavy sticks, the Pirates passed them around, and giving the net an almighty whack, they hurried after Frank.

Frank stopped the car close to the bungalow. 'The moon's as full as it'll ever be,' he said, noticing the green bus snaking up the hillside.

'Quick, Witch Whitely, pass me the Almost Always spell.'

'That's odd... I can't find it anywhere.' Witch Whitely tipped out her bag and began rummaging through the assorted bottles.

'Please hurry! Billy, take off your shoes, and go stand under that tree.' Frank could see the glaring headlights winding upwards in the dark.

'Got it.' Witch Whitely waved the green bottle around. Frank glanced at the moon, and racing to the tree, he sprinkled purple powder over Billy's bare feet.

Billy shot up like a beanstalk as soon as the powder touched his skin. Then as the moon disappeared behind a cloud, he shot down again.

'Look, it's reappearing!' Patsy jumped up and down, pointing to the shimmering, golden ball overhead. Frank sprinkled more powder on Billy's feet, and to everyone's relief, he started to grow.

'Quick, get in the car!' Frank was relieved he'd stopped growing.

'Put on your pyjamas, and act normal,' he said, screeching into the driveway. 'Oh, and tidy your room,' he reminded Billy, seeing the headlights twisting nearer to the bus stop.

Erin's hands were shaking as, very carefully, she tipped the precious Unspell spell into the crystal bottle.

A little, white cloud escaped, and the yellow liquid began to gurgle, fizz and splutter.

'It's ready now,' said the Merrow, and closing her eyes, Erin drank it straight down. Around, and around, she spun, until she was barely visible. Then just when they thought she'd take off; she began to slow down. The spinning finally stopped, and they gasped, to see the figure standing in the moonlight. Gone was the fairy, with the silvery wings, the sparkling wand, and the flowing, silvery gown, and in her place was an old woman, her face lined, and her dark blonde hair flecked with grey. She was wearing old-fashioned, clothes, and although slightly stooped, there was no mistaking the twinkling green eyes behind the half-moon specs.

'Urghhhhhh, you look ghastly! Why on earth do you want to look that old?' cried the Merrow, horrified.

'Gran!' is that really you?' Billy, came hurtling up the country lane in his pyjamas, and threw himself into her arms.

'We did it, William, the spell actually worked! Now I can come home,' she sobbed.

'Thank you so much, Merrow!' they cried, and disgusted, the Merrow turned away.

Frank ran to greet Mary, and Billy's mum, as they got off the bus.

'Well, ladies, I hope you've had a wonderful time,' he said.

'We had a great time. Are you okay?' asked Mary, thinking he looked a bit flustered.

'Great, grand, brilliant,' Frank answered too quickly.

'How did Billy enjoy the fishing trip?' asked his mum.

'Fishing trip?'

'You went on a fishing trip,' she reminded him.

'Silly me. Back a few hours, and forgotten already.' Frank laughed, too loudly.

'Billy's okay, isn't he?'

'Yes, yes, of course. He's missed his mammy though.' Frank was trying to get a grip. 'It's late, you must be tired' he said, grabbing their bags, and shoving them into the boot.

'Mum,' cried Billy, as if he hadn't seen her for a month.

'Well, did you catch a fish for your tea?' his mum smiled.

Billy shook his head. 'We didn't go fishing after all. We were planning a surprise for you, weren't we Frank?' Frank broke into a sweat. What if the spell hadn't worked? He could see Patsy, Ronan, and Tia but where was Billy's gran? Then, he saw her, wearing her half-moon specs, and grinning over Mary's shoulder.

'A surprise for me? How lovely.' cried Billy's mum, turning to see why Frank's mouth was hanging wide open.

'Mum! I don't believe it. This is the best surprise ever. When did you get back? I thought I'd never see you again. You look so tired, and what on earth are you wearing?' Billy's mum grabbed his gran, and squeezed her tight.

'Well, it was a long journey, and there aren't many shops in darkest Peru,' she winked at Billy. 'I promise I'll tell you all about it later.'

'Thank God,' Frank, who was completely overcome with relief, threw his arms around her too.

'Young Billy was pining for his gran,' he told Mary, who was looking at him suspiciously.

'Something's not right around here, and I'm going to find out what it is,' she whispered, in Frank's ear.

'It's a good job she wasn't here ten minutes before,' Patsy whistled.

'What about a nice cuppa?' Mary cuddled Billy's mum, who was sobbing into a tissue.

'Billy, I need your help with the bags,' Frank, ushered him outside.

Witch Whitely was waiting, and tossing a match into the yellow powder, she stood back.

'Fizard's lured the Rat Boys back to the cliff top. He's blocked the secret gap that leads into the cave,' she cackled. Billy didn't understand.

'Fizard is the long-ago wizard, who's responsible for the invisible wall around the cliff top. Now, he's trapped the Rat Boys, and they're prisoners in their own prison. Now the Meadowers don't have to worry about Finbar anymore,' she cackled.

Billy smiled as he watched the images scurrying around in the flames. 'That's brilliant, you mean they're stuck behind that wall forever. You can't miss Duke's big head,' he chuckled, seeing him scrabbling around in the dirt. 'There's Nimrev, too. I knew they'd gnaw their way out of the net. Can't see Finbar, though,' he said, looking closer.

'He was there, and he wasn't looking his best, after his battering in the net,' Witch Whitely cackled.

'Gran wouldn't be coming home if it wasn't for you.' Now back to his normal height, Billy looked down at Witch Whitely.

'Off with you,' she said, wiping away a tear. 'Where are all the others?' Billy patted Grimbleweed's head, and the toad shot out his tongue, and licked his face.

'The Red-Haired Man has gone back to the forest, and the Merrow, to her rock, far out at sea. The Captain and the pirates are keeping an eye on her. You'll see them all before you go home,' Witch Whitely told him.

'Poor Captain Nealy, the Merrow is going to be hard work,' said Billy, chasing the cheeky toad around the garden. 'I'm off too, as soon as Fizard returns on my broomstick. We're great friends now, thanks to Ronan,' she cackled.

'I'm so glad,' said Billy, blowing her a kiss.

Sitting around the kitchen table, they laughed out loud at his gran's made-up tales of darkest Peru. In fact, they were so good, Billy almost believed her.

Then, noticing that Ronan, Patsy and Tia seemed distracted, he turned to see what they were looking at. A snout was pressed firmly against the window pane, and a pair of black, beady eyes, were glinting through the glass.

Finbar's black whiskers twitched in delight. 'It's not over yet, Billy,' he mouthed, through the glass. Billy closed his eyes, and opened them again but he was still smirking through the window. Gran stopped talking halfway through a sentence and Frank let out a loud groan. Drawing his sword, Ronan charged outside and rushing to the window, Billy pulled down the blind.